ROMMEL'S LAST BATTLE

*Leo Kessler titles available from
Severn House Large Print*

The Reich Flies the Flag
Operation Leningrad
Hitler Youth Attacks
Operation Iraq
Kill Patton

ROMMEL'S LAST BATTLE

Leo Kessler

Severn House Large Print
London & New York

This first large print edition published 2009
in Great Britain and the USA by
SEVERN HOUSE PUBLISHERS LTD of
9-15 High Street, Sutton, Surrey, SM1 1DF.
First world regular print edition published 2006 by
Severn House Publishers Ltd., London and New York.

British Library Cataloguing in Publication Data

Kessler, Leo, 1926-
    Rommel's last battle. - Large print ed. - (S.S. Wotan
    series)
    1. Rommel, Erwin, 1891-1944 - Fiction 2. World War,
    1939-1945 - Campaigns - Africa, North - Fiction 3. War
    stories 4. Large type books
    I. Title
    823.9'14[F]

    ISBN-13: 978-0-7278-7751-2

Printed and bound in Great Britain by
MPG Books Ltd, Bodmin, Cornwall

'When we are old and wear dark, baggy suits and slightly greasy bowler hats ... we'll order more beer and begin painting this bitchy trull of a war until it looks like a latter-day saint.'

Cassandra (aka W. Connor), 1943

Author's Note

The English made the 'Desert Fox', the German Field Marshal Erwin Rommel. Without the English, the little Swabian with the country accent might well have been as obscure as the other talented German commanders of the same rank. They fought tremendous battles with three or four times the number of divisions under Rommel's command. But they fought in Russia against the 'Ivans', where the war might be won by Hitler, but where it was ultimately lost. For in the end, it was 'Ivans', as we called them on the Eastern Front, who beat National Socialist Germany, and not the Anglo-Americans.

Rommel, however, fought against the 'Tommies' for two years and beat them time and time again. For the most part of those years he commanded just a handful of divisions, and when he fought the Americans in his last battle, he beat the US Army too, with just a single German panzer division.

Thus for the British and later for the unfortunate *Amis*, Rommel became the most brilliant German field commander – a legend in his own time. In 1942, for instance, his British opposite number Sir Claude Auchinleck, commander of his country's long-suffering 8th Army, wrote in a memo to his senior commanders and warned them: 'There is a real danger that our friend Rommel will turn into a bogeyman for our troops just because they talk so much about him. He is *not* superhuman.' Auchinleck added a postscript: 'I am not jealous of Rommel.'

But he was, and in the end he had to go after yet another defeat at the hands of the 'Desert Fox'. Auchinleck's successor who would finally defeat 'the living legend', General Montgomery, might not have been jealous of Rommel, but he was definitely worried by him. He kept a picture of Rommel permanently in his front line caravan. He said it was because he wanted to look at it and try to figure out 'what new rabbit' the German would 'pull out of the hat'.

Rommel's fellow German field marshals were not impressed by the 'Desert Fox', despite the reputation the English had foisted on him. Field Marshal Gerd von Rundstedt thought of him as 'just a good divisional commander but no more than that'.

But that was during the war. After the war, in a defeated Germany, the Rommel cult, which the English had created, started anew. A destroyer in the new West German fleet was named after the 'Desert Fox'. Several new army barracks bearing his name followed. Streets everywhere were similarly named *'Rommelstrasse'*. Anglo-American movies, usually with English actors such as James Mason and the like playing the great general, the epitome of the new German democratic soldier, were shown in West German cinemas everywhere. Rommel was now a German *Volksheld*, a 'People's Hero'.

But for some the 'Desert Fox' was still a traitor who had betrayed the Führer and who had intended to assassinate him, stabbing the *Vaterland* in the back just as the Jews and Socialists had done in the First World War. For in the end, in 1944, it was not the English or the Americans who had gotten rid of the German bogeyman they had created (though in that same year the English had planned to eliminate Rommel by force until they learned of the real game he was playing behind Hitler's back). It was the Germans themselves. For after fighting – *and winning* – his last battle in North Africa, Rommel turned traitor to the system which had given him the power to become the legend the

English had created. For that, in National Socialist Germany he had to pay the ultimate penalty – *death!*

This then is the story of *Rommel's Last Battle*...

Leo Kessler,
Bayrisch-Gmain, Bavaria,
Summer 2005.

BRANDENBURGERS ATTACK!

'What will history say in passing its verdict on me? If I am successful here, then everybody else will claim the glory. But if I fail, then everybody will be after my blood.'
                                        The Rommel Diary

Highway One, South, Sfax, Tunisia,
Dec 22nd 1942

Oberleutnant Scharf had heard it all before. Many times. Bits he understood. Most he didn't. Still he listened out of habit. Head cocked to one side, ignoring the chatter of his Brandenburgers behind in the body of the Junkers, he took in the *Luftwaffe* pilot's crisp instructions.

'*Brakes locked ... Elevators trim ... two points back ... Pitch fully fine Flaps-check...*' Now the twin engines of the old 'Auntie Ju', as his Brandenburgers called the antiquated transport plane, were going all out. The men ceased talking. It was too difficult to hear each other. The fuselage started to tremble. It was like some domestic animal straining to be let off the leash and gain its freedom of action.

The first pilot continued his traditional litany for the sake of the co-pilot. '*Trim set for straight and level flight ... Two hundred kilometres an hour. Attention to chocs...*' The noise

11

rose to an ear-splitting fury. Behind them they threw up a wake of thick white sand which had, as usual, drifted across the desert road overnight.

Hurriedly the fresh-faced young co-pilot thrust his head through the open side window of the cockpit and yelled at the two mechanics waiting below, 'Chocs away!'

Expertly dodging the whirling radial engines, they darted beneath the quickening blades, overalls immediately splattered by oil from above, and moved backwards, dragging the ropes attached to the chocs behind them. Scharf forced a grin, as he always did at this stage. It was meant to encourage his men, though most of his Brandenburgers were 'old hares' who had been in this sort of a thing often enough before.

Relieved of the last restraint, the pilot eased the joystick forward and the heavily laden transport started to roll along the dead-straight desert road. Time and time again it bounced as its wheels hit a pothole or a badly filled-in shell crater. The Junkers gathered more speed. Scharf felt a quickening of his senses. They were on their way into the unknown; there was no turning back now. He threw a glance out of the tiny window. He caught a glimpse of the plane's shadow. In a second they'd be airborne. Then they were, and were climbing as fast as the Junkers could rise.

Below, the featureless desert, littered here and there with the wrecked tanks of the year's fighting, started to recede. An Arab on a camel halted his beast and, shading his eyes out of habit, stared up at the heavily laden plane, and then he and the desert were gone abruptly and they were flying towards the sun. The cabin was flooded with bright yellow light, and Scharf's hard, bronzed face relaxed. He was filled with a new sense of hope. He guessed it was the sight of the sun in this gloomy December of defeat for German arms in Africa.

He flung a glance behind him at his Brandenburgers. They were relaxing too, even the 'nervous nellies' among them who still didn't like flying. Here and there they were lighting up their 'cancer sticks' without permission. Others had pulled their rimless parachutists' helmets down over their eyes and were attempting to sleep, lulled by the steady drone of the 'Auntie Ju's' engines. A couple, again contrary to *Wehrmacht* regulations, were sipping from their water bottles, containing the native *'arak'*★ instead of the customary water or cold tea.

Scharf shrugged. It didn't matter. His

★*A native alcohol usually made from the date palm.*

13

Brandenburgers no longer concerned themselves with regulations. They were doomed men and they knew it. As they quipped among themselves, 'Enjoy the war, the peace is going to be terrible.' Not that most of them would ever see the end of the war.

Even as he looked around at their tough brown faces underneath the cropped hair, he told himself there were only a handful of them left, those men whom he had first led into action in Poland back in '39, in what now seemed another age. The rest had long perished in Holland, France, Greece, Russia and on half a dozen other battlefields spread all over Europe.

Scharf frowned and turned back to his front. He opened his silver cigarette case and helped himself to one of his precious Woodbines, acquired from a Tommy supply dump near Tobruk they had looted during the previous month's raid. He breathed in the rich Virginia aroma and felt a little dizzy for a moment. After the kind of 'lung torpedoes' that the 'supply bulls' of the Wehrmacht provided for the troops, the Tommy cigarettes were really a heady luxury.

He forgot the cigarettes and concentrated on the problem on hand. He guessed this wasn't going to be one of the usual daring, if routine, Brandenburg missions: a raid or act of sabotage far behind enemy lines, with the troops being flown in and then, with the enemy at their heels, trying to make their way back to their own lines on foot. After all, it wasn't every day that he was briefed by no less a person than the commander of the *Afrikakorps*. Even now with his reputation shot, his troops defeated time and time again by that little Tommy in his baggy shorts and funny hats, Montgomery, and out of favour with the Führer himself, the 'Desert Fox' was an important, even legendary figure.

Scharf closed his eyes momentarily. He wasn't tired. He was instead thinking of that day back in May '40 when he had first met him, and how different he had been then...

Dasburg, Germany, May 9th 1940

The fat maid had come stomping up the stairs of their billet next to the ruined castle at the border village which had given the godforsaken place its name. Scharf woke up immediately, his mind already full of the importance of the day to come. She'd be bringing up his breakfast as ordered. He had told her to find him something special. After all, 'I'm about to die for Folk, Fatherland, and Führer.'

'I'll do my best, Mr Officer,' she'd replied dutifully in her trusting peasant fashion. 'I'll see if I can get you a nice piece of *speck* from the farm.'

He had grinned. He'd had other things in

mind than a chunk of salty local bacon for his breakfast.

Now, as below in the shadow of the castle on the height overlooking the Belgian border river his men stripped to the waist, washed noisily and ate their breakfast ration of a half a litre of 'gidding soup' made from dried peas and horsemeat, he felt below the duvet for his erection. It was as stiff as a cop's truncheon. It'd be a nice breakfast surprise for the fat, slow peasant maid. He licked his lips in anticipation, and it was not at the thought of the dried bacon; he had another piece of fresh, juicier meat in mind.

Politely, she had knocked, and after a pause entered. She curtsied as was the fashion of such humble girls in the presence of a *Herr Offizier*. In her red big paws she had held his breakfast tray, complete with a flower plucked in the meadow.

'*Guten Morgen, Herr Leutnant*,' she had announced. '*Ihr Frühstück*.'

His *Frühstück*, breakfast, had been far from his mind that fateful May morning so long before. But he had contained his excitement. Quietly he commanded, 'Please put it on the side cupboard and come over here.'

She had done as he had ordered and crossed the room to his big, old-fashioned bed slowly, almost as if she had guessed what was coming. She stopped, and in the cheeky fashion of his youth before the war had hardened him into a sombre, careful man, he said 'Want to bring me luck, girl?'

'Bring you luck sir? But how, *Herr Leutnant?*'

He pulled back the covers to reveal his erect penis, red and swollen. 'With this. Who knows where I might be tomorrow? Looking at the potatoes from beneath two metres of earth.'

She nodded her head in that slow peasant fashion and said, 'I understand, sir ... But you'll be careful.'

Outside near the ruined medieval castle, one of the Brandenburg NCOs was shouting, 'All right, you bunch o' piss pansies. Stop feeding yer ugly mugs. You've had 'em in the trough long enough, get fell in.'

Abruptly Scharf had realized that time was running out fast. He'd have to be quick if he was going to make the two-backed beast with the girl. *'Los,'* he said. 'Are you ready?'

She sighed a little, as if she realized that this was going to be her fate. Letting men stick it into her. 'It's big,' she murmured.

'I aim to please. Come on.'

She turned and pulled her skirt up to reveal patched but clean white cotton knickers that came down halfway to her thighs. He had shaken his head. They weren't exactly pants that would turn a man on. But in his present condition, he couldn't be overly particular. Without any further orders, she reached down and pulled them off. Then she held on to the cupboard and looked up at the crucifix and the cheap, garish portrait of the Last Supper, which was the little inn bedroom's sole decoration. 'I'm ready, sir,' she said. 'But careful—'

'I'll pull it out before I come,' he had reassured her, lying even as he said the words. What did the future matter now? He might well be dead, lying in some bloody Belgian ditch before the morrow was out. A fighting soldier had to take his pleasures as they came, without worrying about the consequences.

Lightly he sprang out of the big bed, body all muscle, not one bit of fat on it; his long training had seen to that. Hurriedly, he positioned himself behind her. 'Hold tight,' he said cheerfully, breath coming a little faster, as if he were some conductor on the underground in his native Berlin.

The girl started to mutter a prayer. He thought it was 'Hail Mary'. They were very Catholic here in this remote German border country.

'Yes, say your prayers, Fräulein,' he said to himself. Then with a grunt he thrust himself into her, grasping her heavy flanks tightly as he did so. She gasped. Below, the NCOs were calling, *'Erste Kompanie – hierüber Dalli ... dalli ...* Let's be having you now, you lot of asparagus Tarzans.' Everywhere there was noise, the stamp of hobnailed boots, the clatter of equipment, the brass-shod butts of rifles hitting the cobbles of the winding road that led down to the river, which they would soon cross, and then it would all begin.

But Scharf didn't hear the noise. Now the coming battle had been forgotten. All he was concerned with was the satisfaction of his lust, his own pleasures. But that day in May 1940, *Leutnant* Scharf was fated not to complete his encounter with the simple country serving girl. Abruptly, a stern, urgent order broke into his wild sexual reverie. *'Achtung,'* a harsh voice below cried. 'General officer approaching ... *stillgestanden.'*

Scharf, his sweat-lathered body working back and forth furiously, tried to ignore the sudden alarm near the ruined castle. But he couldn't. A moment later, the order was followed by the nailed stamp of jackboots hitting the cobbles as one and the voice of a senior NCO yelling, *'Herr General, melde gehorsam zwanzig Mann und ein Feldwebel zur Stelle...'*

Scharf cursed. He didn't wait to hear the rest of the traditional report to a superior officer. He sprang up as if some damned great hornet had just stung his naked buttocks. The girl didn't hear the sucking noise as he withdrew from her. She continued working her haunches in and out excitedly for a few seconds more before she realized that he was no longer making love to her. 'What ... what is it, sir?' she gasped, stopping slowly, as if she could not comprehend why he was no longer between her thighs.

'*What is it?*' he echoed in angry frustration. 'Holy strawsack, what the shit do you think, you stupid cow? ... It's the damned general, woman.' Then he forgot her, as he pulled on his breeches and tunic while she still grasped the cupboard, her skirt thrown up over her naked buttocks. Cursing and fuming, he stumbled down the creaking wooden stairs, trying to pull on his boots as he did so.

Thus he had met the unknown general for the very first time: the one who was soon destined to become as famous throughout the Reich as any handsome USA movie star.

The general was standing with his back to him as Scharf emerged from the inn, tugging on his helmet. He was ignoring the soldiers standing stiffly to attention with the sergeant still clasping his right hand to his helmet in salute. Instead he was standing down at the little River Our below, which separated the Reich from neutral Belgium. There was a thoughtful look on his bold, broad face with its pugnacious, aggressive jaw. It was the face of a born soldier, Scharf had told himself at that moment. This unknown tank general who was to command the follow-up attack, once he and his Brandenburgers had seized the bridge spanning the river and steep wooden heights of the Ardennes beyond, was not one of those intellectual Prussian aristocrats who commanded their men from some chateau far behind the lines. His very presence here this dawn proved that.

Suddenly the strange general swung round as Scharf clicked to attention and commenced reporting. But the general with the tough face and the highest imperial award for bravery, the *Pour le Mérite*, dangling from his neck, had interrupted with a curt, 'Herr Leutnant, who are these Brandenburgers of yours? I have searched the Army List. There is no mention of them.'

'They are the special troops of the *Abwehr*'s* special operations department, sir. They are all volunteers, recruited from Germans who have lived abroad and speak foreign languages, and others from friendly nations who have volunteered, too, to fight for Germany's cause, sir.' He saw by the look on the general's face he had said enough. He was an officer in a hurry. He didn't need any unnecessary explanations.

German Secret Service.

21

'Volunteers, eh,' the general mused for a moment, then he slapped the cane he affected against his leg sharply. 'Excellent. All right. You may dismiss. My tanks will expect to roll across the Our and up those damned steep heights by six hundred hours tomorrow morning, the tenth of May.' With that, he turned and strode back purposefully to his waiting staff car. But before his motorcycle escort had managed to turn and follow the camouflaged Horch racing back to the main road at top speed, Scharf had managed to stop one of the motorcyclists and ask, 'Corporal, what's the name of your general, eh?'

The man had grinned in the fashion of old soldiers who had seen it all before – and then some – before answering, 'God in heaven, sir, I hardly know it myself. He's allus on the move. *Rommel*, sir, that's his moniker ... General Wilhlem, no, wait a minute, General *Erwin* Rommel, that's it. Flying Frigging Rommel, if you'll excuse the language.'

And with that he had pulled down his goggles, pressed on the pedal. With a roar and screech of burning rubber, he was off, chasing the fast-disappearing staff car, leaving Scharf staring after him and his 'flying frigging Rommel'...

As the old transport plane, packed with his

Brandenburgs, droned ever closer to their drop zone on the border between Tunisia and Libya, Scharf remembered the Rommel of that first day and mentally compared him with the 'Desert Fox', the Field Marshal Rommel who had given him his orders for this mission only twenty-four hours before.

What a change had taken place in the man between that May day and now, after the *Afrikakorps* commander had spent two years fighting the Tommies in the Western Desert. Indeed, Scharf hardly recognized the Field Marshal, he looked so old, worn and ill, his face and lips covered in desert sores, his skin yellow with jaundice.

Wearily Rommel had drawn a line in the sand with his fly whisk and said in a cracked voice, as if he had been drinking too much, 'Here the Tommies dug in, in what they call the Mareth Line. The English have learned. Montgomery might be slow...'

But Scharf had not really been listening to his exposition. He was too alarmed by the commander's appearance and lacklustre tone. He seemed to have lost all his old enthusiasm for combat – and his confidence. He was a commander who appeared to be going through the motions.

He had forced himself to listen again as Rommel continued. 'But he'll attack in the end, and we won't, in the long run, be able to hold him. After all, Scharf, most of my troops are Macaronis' – he meant Italians, '– and we both know what their value is.' He shrugged wearily like a man who was sorely tried. 'So what is left for us to do?' He answered his own question. 'We must postpone the inevitable.'

Scharf had told himself it was time for him to ask something, and he did. 'How, sir?'

Rommel pointed with his stick at the line he had drawn in the sand. 'The Tommy front stretches from the sea to the sand dunes down to the south-west, and they are virtually impassable, especially for armour. So we can guess Montgomery will attack from somewhere along that twenty-two-kilometre-long front, and he will attack where he has his best troops stationed at this moment. He won't have the time to do any juggling.'

Again Scharf thought it time to ask another brief question and help the obviously exhausted Field Marshal. 'So we find out where those best troops are currently dug in, sir?' he suggested.

Surprisingly enough, Rommel suddenly displayed some of his old sparkle. He laughed, showing his blackened, rotting teeth, and said, 'My dear young man, I can see that you are not cut out to wear the red stripe of the Greater German General Staff on your breeches. Good commanders never do the obvious, you know.'

'Sir?'

'No, in this case they do not attempt to discover where the enemy's strongest troops are located. Why give away your intentions? For an Englishman, Montgomery is quite intelligent. He'd soon tumble to my plan. No, that is *not* what I want you to do.'

'What is then, sir?'

Rommel had not been angered at his boldness. Instead he had pulled Scharf closer to him, as if he might be afraid of being overheard even by his own personal staff. He was so close then that Scharf had flinched at the foul, fetid smell that had come from his mouth, as if there was something nasty rotting inside the Field Marshal's guts. 'We – *you* – do this...'

Wadi Zigzaou, Libya, Dec 24th 1942

They lay in the scrub and camel thorn. It was cold, and they were all awake. Huddled in their sleeping bags, they listened to the old familiar noise of the desert. Hands propped beneath their heads as they lay there, staring at the brilliant silver sky, the stars so close that they felt they could reach up and grab one, they listened to the 'singing of the sand'. It was the millions of sand grains, rubbing and contracting against one another in the night cold after the heat of the day, giving off a strange haunting keening.

Half a kilometre to their front lay the enemy positions. They were silent too, save the solitary crunch of a sentry's boots in the freezing sand, and once or twice the hiss of a match, followed by a spurt of blue flame as the sentry lit an illegal cigarette and smoked it cupped in the palm of his hand. It was clear that the enemy didn't know that they were out here in the yellow waste, or expect any trouble on this particular day. After all it was their Christmas Eve, and this night the Tommies would be receiving an extra rum ration and a steaming portion of that celebrated Christmas pudding of theirs. Captain Scharf licked his sand-cracked lips at the thought of the rum. He certainly could have done with a stiff hot drink at this moment.

The young officer dismissed the idle thought. There was no time to be wasted on such matters. Christmas or not, there were other things to be done this morning. Indeed, in a way the date was opportune. The Tommies wouldn't expect trouble on this day of all days. What Christian would want a fight on Christmas Eve?

He chuckled slightly at the thought. But then the enemy opposite him, he told himself, wasn't Christian. They were soldiers of the Indian Army, Hindus or Muslims or something like that, who didn't drink, poor shits, or so he had been informed.

For the last two days since they had been dropped by the 'Auntie Ju' at the DZ prepared for them by Arabs in the *Abwehr*'s pay, they had ranged the British front at Mareth. They had marched during the night, lain up by day, secretly surveying the enemy positions. They had used all their knowledge and experience of the desert war to ascertain at a distance what kind of troops they were facing. They had soon discovered that those closest to the sea were New Zealanders, the toughest soldiers in the enemy force. They had been easy to make out. They were the only Allied troops supplied with mutton from their homeland, and there was no mistaking the smell of smoked, boiled mutton, wafted on the desert breeze at night when all the troops, German and British, cooked their main meal of the day.

The Australians had been next. They had been even easier to ascertain and identity. They made so much noise. He knew from past experience that the tall, rangy men from that far continent were fine fighters, but awfully boastful and loud. They and the New Zealanders were obviously going to be the English general Montgomery's assault force when the time came for him to attack. The

Poles had followed. Like most Germans of his generation, Scharf had started the war feeling only contempt for those third-rate Slavs. In Poland the *Wehrmacht* had gone through their army like a hot knife through butter. But over the years he had changed his opinion, and he had learned to respect the Poles' fighting ability. They were a dour, hardy force, embued with a fierce hatred of the Germans. But they were poorly armed by the British, and poorly led. They'd be devils in defence, but he didn't think that Montgomery would use them to lead any attack.

These black soldiers from India, as he thought of them, whom he observed now, were the most likely candidates. After all, hadn't Rommel maintained scornfully that you couldn't expect much from soldiers who wouldn't even harm an insect. 'It's against their religion, I believe, Scharf,' he had explained. 'In three devils' names, they won't even kill a desert scorpion, man, and we both know what terrible insects they are.'

Now Scharf whispered to Sergeant Hartmann, formerly of the Foreign Legion and a real old desert hand, 'All right, Hartmann, raise their bodies, we're going forward at zero seven hundred. They'll be eating then,' he added, sniffing the air and noting the pungent smell of the native cooking.

Hartmann, big, burly and brutal-faced, pulled himself out of his sleeping bag, revealing the old legend tattooed around his sun-browned neck, *'SLIT HERE'*. He grinned momentarily. 'I'd rather have a crack at the Tommies, sir. They had firewater a man can loot. Those Indians, why, they don't even have cancer sticks, even if they are made of camel shit, that a man can loot.'

Scharf had long given up trying to convince Hartmann that he was in the *Wehrmacht* to fight for 'Folk, Fatherland and Führer' and not to indulge in his taste for exotic foreign whores and the paint stripper that he called 'firewater'. Instead he shrugged slightly, and added, 'And tell the men that I'll cut the eggs off any trooper who makes a noise. I want this to be silent and as painless as possible. In and out with no casualties.'

Hartmann's brutal grin broadened even more. He liked the bit about 'cutting the eggs off'. He said, 'And I'll help you do it, sir – *with a blunt razor blade.*' Then he was off, crawling from man to man with surprising speed for such a big man, gently placing his ham-like fist over their mouths as he woke them in order to prevent them making the slightest sound at being awakened so suddenly.

Scharf watched him go for a moment

before rolling out of the warmth of his own sleeping bag, shuddering a little in the cold, mind already full of what he had to do in order to carry out his part in Rommel's plan...

A quarter of a mile away, Colonel 'Crasher' Nichols of the Army's Intelligence Corps lay awake in his own sleeping bag, pondering Rommel's plan too – or what the clever-featured young ex-don thought Rommel's plan might be. For Nicols represented a school of thought not particularly popular at Montgomery's forward desert HQ. *He* expected Rommel to launch a spoiling attack on the Mareth Line, whereas the current top brass opinion was that the Germans had shot their bolt. Once Monty attacked with his superior force, so the official view went, the Huns would undertake another retreat, simply trying to slow down the 'Master's' advance, but not attempting to stand and make a major battle of it. 'God Almighty, Crasher,' his superior, the regular army brigadier, had snapped testily when he had mentioned his own thoughts on the subject once again during the latest intelligence conference back in Cairo, 'how long do you want this bloody campaign to go on for? Rommel and his sodding *Afrikakorps* has been holding us up too bloody long as it is.

Let's drive him into the bloody Med and get back home. I haven't seen England or played a decent game of cricket for two bloody long years now. It's more than a chap can bear, Crasher.' The brigadier had glared at the young colonel with his tortoise glasses and bland innocent face as if he still couldn't believe that this mild-mannered man, who looked more like a public schoolboy from a minor school than a half-colonel in the British Army, could be regarded by some in high places as one of the best intelligence officers in the whole of Monty's Eighth Army.

It had been after that particular conference that Nichols had suggested he should motor down to the Mareth Line and put his theories to test; attempt to discover if the Germans had the strength to counter-attack, and where they might do so if they had that strength.

As usual, Nichols's keen academic mind had soon sorted out what the defenders' problem might well be if Rommel did have the strength to attack. It was clear to him that the *Afrikakorps*, even when supported by Italian armour, didn't have the ability to outflank Montgomery successfully any more, as Rommel had done so often in the past. Instead, any assault launched on the Mareth Line by the Germans would be aimed at disrupting the Eighth Army assault as soon as it started, and forcing Monty to slow down, even stop the main drive. And where might that German attack come? In the manner of lonely men, Nichols talked to himself when he ruminated over his problems. 'The Indians, of course,' he had concluded a couple of days before. 'They're the weakest spot, and old Rommel has a nasty talent for finding our bloody weak spots, even now when he's on his uppers.'

His findings since he had arrived at the Indian Brigade HQ, here in the centre of the Line, had seemed to bear out his theories. The Indians were mostly new recruits straight from the depots back in the subcontinent, poorly trained and armed, and although they were all volunteers like their now long-dead or captured predecessors, they were disaffected, influenced by the general anti-British attitude of the native politicians back home. Already some three thousand of their captured predecessors in German hands had been formed into a German Army brigade, the 'Indian Legion', released from the Reich's POW camps to be trained and armed by the enemy, and prepared to fight against their former colonial masters. Thus it was that Nichols suspected, from the various murmurings and rumours he had picked up around the Indian HQ, that if Rommel attacked, the Indian Brigade might not be so steadfast as it should be. 'Indeed, old chap,' he had told himself in that funny manner of his, 'they might well pick up their boots and scarper.' For that reason, he was going to have an early breakfast this Christmas Eve, so that he could spend it with the British Royal Artillery regiment which supported the Indian Brigade. But it wasn't the high jinks, Christmas pud and, with a bit of luck, a decent whisky toddy, which attracted him to the British gunners. It was instead the chance to put them on guard, just in case his suspicions proved true. Their twenty-five pounder guns might well save the day, if the worst came to the worst.

So the ex-don, with his mild manner and shy liking for handsome young men with long locks of hair hanging down over their foreheads in the Christopher Isherwood fashion, clapped his hands to summon his temporary Indian batman with his hot shaving water and dreadful Indian-style porridge, and prepared to meet the gunners. They'd be undoubtedly very regimental and British Army – 'if it moves, salute it; if it don't, whitewash it,' he chuckled to himself. 'And bullshit reigns supreme.' It wouldn't do to be incorrectly dressed when he met their CO...

Things were going well, Scharf told himself. His 'old hares' were doing everything he expected of them. There'd be no need for Hartmann's help with his 'blunt razorblade' to carry out that threatened punishment if any one of the veterans slipped up. They were moving forward towards the unsuspecting Indians noiselessly, taking advantage of every little bit of cover, avoiding kicking up the slightest cloud of sand each time they made another move. Scharf smiled momentarily. With luck, he could carry out the mission Rommel had given him and escape without loss.

It seemed too that the weather was in his favour. The night's freezing cold had given way to a surprisingly hot dawn. It could have been a furnace-hot day in the African summer. Now the sky was the colour of wood smoke. No wind stirred. The sun was like a coin seen dimly at the bottom of a dirty pond. It felt as if a storm was approaching, unusual at this time of the year.

Still, Scharf was too busy with the task at hand to concern himself greatly with that possibility. For already, the two machine gun teams on both left and right flanks were close to the Indians' wire. Once they were in position, he'd start the operation from the centre where he and Hartmann were now.

With a bit of luck, they would frighten the Indians into revealing their positions, strength and ability to react. Then, while the centre retreated safely, the two MG teams on the flanks would give them covering fire and keep the Indians, if they were bold enough to do so, from following the retreating Brandenburgers. So he crawled on together with the rest. Like predatory brown timber wolves, they closed on the unsuspecting Indians, busy with their tea and the funny pancakes that he was told they ate for breakfast instead of a good old bowl of 'fart soup', made from peas, complete with 'turd', i.e. sausage, that his own old hares loved.

But now Scharf felt himself sweating profusely. As usual in the desert when a soldier sweated, the flies appeared from nowhere and commenced their maddening buzzing as they got into his ears and eyes. He was sorely tempted to curse out loud at them. He contained his annoyance, limiting himself to an odd sotto voce 'damned shit' as the twin machine gun teams, dimly visible in the heat haze now, started setting up their machine guns, the gunners draped in long belts of ammunition.

He peered to his front through the thickening air. Still smoke from the Indians' cooking fires was rising up slowly. He could just smell the pungent, acrid odour of their

spices, but it was becoming ever more difficult to do so. He knew why. The air pressure
was increasing rapidly. The storm was on its
way. It was time to act. He cursed and
remembered the old Senussi saying at such
moments, 'Death is a black camel which
kneels at every man's door'. Now they'd be
facing up to something that was more des-
tructive, if you were unlucky, than any
artillery barrage. Soon, he told himself, the
old Arab saying would come true, the black
camel would be kneeling at the door of his
Brandenburgers. His mind made up, he rose
to his feet, exposing himself fully, but no
longer caring that he was doing so. '*Los*,' he
cried in the very same instant that the great
gust of wind came howling down along the
desert plain out of nowhere...

'Oh my sainted aunt,' Crasher Nichols cursed in that mild fashion of his as the searingly
hot wind struck the jeep and stopped it
dead. In front, the havildar driving it slammed into the windscreen and yelped with
pain as the blood started to spurt from his
broken nose in a bright red sparkling arc.
Nichols grabbed him by the collar and, with
surprising strength for such a skinny man,
pulled him to the ground. Just in time. A
moment later, another tremendous blast of
that monstrous, furnace-hot wind slammed

into the little vehicle and tossed it on its side like a child's toy.

But even as the wind struck home, Nichols heard that well-remembered sound: the high-pitched, almost hysterical burr of a German MG 42, firing all out, over a thousand rounds a minute. They were being attacked.

He pulled the corporal's rifle from the bucket slot at the side of the overturned jeep, its engine still running despite everything, and began to work his way forward to the sound of the firing, muted every now and again as that hundred mph wind struck home time and time again.

It felt as if he were trying to climb the face of Mount Everest. He could only manage a step at a time, using all the strength of his frail body to do even that. The wind struck his face and frame with lethal ferocity. He felt he might be swept off his feet and bowled off into the unknown like the camel's thorn skidding by him on all sides. Sand particles struck through his thin khaki shirt. They hit his face with razor-like sharpness, as if someone was prodding his skin with the point of a stiletto. Now and again, he opened his mouth to howl with pain, but that tremendous, awe-inspiring wind snatched the sounds from it.

Breathing became difficult. He choked like

an ancient asthmatic in the throes of a fatal attack. Above his bent head, his hair full of sand, his cap long blown away, the undulating threnody of the storm rose to an ever louder pitch. It had blown a thousand miles across the desert to strike them, friend and foe alike, and it was not going to be denied its victims.

Over and over again it battered him and the rest with its giant fist. Tents flew by him; bodies, dead or alive, he could not even guess, did so too. Once, in a fleeting pause, Nichols forced his bent head up and blinked the sand caked on them. He thought he glimpsed dark outlines in an unfamiliar uniform before him to the right. He fired instinctively from the hip. Surprisingly, the Indian corporal Lee-Enfield rifle still worked. A blast of flame. A groan. The figure seemed to crumple. Next moment, the wind descended upon them once more with renewed vigour. He ducked his head fearfully.

Now the wind shrieked and wailed hideously. It was as if some grotesque figure had been sent by God on high who had ordained that these puny, war-loving mortals should be wiped off the face of the earth once and for all. Why, they had to be punished because of their temerity in penetrating his burning, solitary kingdom of sand.

For minutes on end, 'Crasher' Nichols thought he might go mad. He was alone in this crazy, howling world of flying sand. Why should he survive? But he kept his head. He knew that out there, somewhere in the midst of this mad maelstrom, there was the enemy – and the enemy had to be dealt with. It seemed that only he could deal with them before it was too late. For the Indians had vanished, almost as if they had not been there in the first place. Grimly, body bent almost double, he straggled on. Then he heard what he sought: the crackle of a wireless set, the command net, he prayed and hoped. For in the same instant that he heard the radio, he heard, too, the hiss of German machine gun fire, and what he took to be commands in that language. The Germans, with their usual tough doggedness, had not retreated before that terrible sandstorm. He had to deal with them before they penetrated the Indian Brigade's line in depth, if that was their intention. Eyes narrowed to slits, he felt his way, one hand outstretched like that of a blind man, for the radio tent...

Scharf cursed yet again. He cursed the desert, the storm and the blacks for not showing themselves, if they were really hiding, and surrendering so that he could interrogate them and find out the information that Field Marshal Rommel wanted so desperately. Then he could take his damned hind legs in his hands and do a bunk toot sweet, before the balloon went up and he found himself in the desert without a bit of cover once the storm had abated.

Still, as far as he could ascertain in the middle of this mad whirling chaos, his Brandenburgers were doing well. Muted but definite, he could hear their cries of delight as they looted the vanished Indian officers' tents and found illegal whisky and gin, with which they were issued like their white comrades of field rank were. Hartmann and his 'old hares' wouldn't pass up a chance to knock back such delightful firewater, even in the midst of a battle, he knew that.

All the same, Scharf was not sure that he had found the weak spot in the British line that Rommel sought for his spoiling attack. If he couldn't, and was forced to inform Rommel of his lack of success, he wondered for a moment or two what alternative there was left for the ailing 'Desert Fox'. Now, however, he dismissed that worrying thought from his mind for the time being. Despite the damned storm and the confusion it had caused to his attack, he had to continue forward and discover what was the true state of the Indian Brigade. It was risky, he knew. All the same, so far there had been no real reaction from the enemy's native troops, and from what he could tell from Hartmann and his bunch of hard-boiled looters, they were encountering no real resistance to speak of. Scharf gripped his pistol more firmly in his sweaty hand and, bent double, eyes narrowed to slits against the howling wind and the whirling sand, he pushed on once more.

'Crasher' Nichols dived into the radio tent, gasping for breath, grateful to be out of the storm, although the canvas of the frail structure billowed in and out wildly with every gust as if it might blow away at any moment.

The tent was empty, signal forms strewn everywhere among the secret code books. A rifle lay in the sand of the floor, as if its unknown owner might have been about to use it when the Germans had attacked, and had then changed his mind and run away. 'Crasher' cursed and snorted. 'What a bloody unholy mess.' He forgot the vanished Indian signallers and flashed a glance at the command radio. The red light glowed on the set. He whistled softly. It was still working. 'Thank God,' he exclaimed, again talking to himself.

For a former don, whose speciality had been 'Middle High German' and the post-Lutte form of German, he was surprisingly up to date in modern technology. Indeed, he

had often surprised his colleagues at con-
ferences with his knowledge of technical
military procedures, radio procedures, gun
trajectories, ranges and the like. Now he
knew exactly what to do. As he bent over the
radio, blowing away the sand which almost
covered it, he said aloud, 'It's going to be
damned dangerous. But it's the only way.'

Naturally, he knew the Indian Brigade's
call sign without referring to the signal notes
pinned behind the radio, now flapping up
and down in that tremendous wind. He
knew the co-ordinates of their HQ as well.
As outside he could hear the cries and calls
in German which indicated the attackers
were coming closer, he bent and, attaching
the earphones, twirled the radio's dials hastily. '*LOS ... MANNER*,' a harsh voice was
yelling, only yards away, '*WOLLT IHR HIER
KREPIEREN?*'

The bespectacled intelligence colonel
pulled a face. If the British gunners didn't
respond immediately the only one around
here who would be 'croaking' might well be
him. His free hand fumbled hastily for his
revolver, but still he worked urgently on the
radio. He had only seconds left before the
Germans came blundering into the signals
tent, a key objective for them if they were
looking for intelligence.

There it was through the buzz of static

and urgent messages being flashed back and forth, reporting storm damage and the like. He wasted no time. Hurriedly, he gave the brigade call sign. It was acknowledged almost immediately. Outside, someone was fumbling with the tangled opening flap of the tent. Nichols pulled out his revolver and clicked off the safety catch.

The voice of the artillery operator at the other end came through suddenly loud and clear. It was almost too much for 'Crasher' Nichols. He started. It must have startled the unknown German outside. He shouted something. Nichols wasted no further time. He snapped out the camp's co-ordinates. This was a desperate situation and it needed desperate solutions. He was going to bring down the 25-pounders' massed fire on the Indians' camp and risk being blown to smithereens himself.

The flap opened. He swung round and fired in the very same instant. A big German in the peaked cap and bleached uniform of the *Afrikakorps* paused there for what seemed a long time, mouth open stupidly, as the blood started to stain his tunic. Sluggishly, almost as if in slow motion, his big hand crept up to his stomach. He winced as they were covered immediately with his own blood. He looked down in disbelief, as if he couldn't comprehend that this terrible thing was happening to him. His guts were starting to ooze from his shattered stomach, slithering out snake-like, grey-pink and steaming. A moan of absolute agony began to form on his abruptly bloodless lips.

Nichols didn't give him a chance to utter it. For such a mild-looking man, he was suddenly very hard and decisive. He fired again. At that range, he couldn't miss. The dying German was propelled through the flap of the tent, as if punched by some giant fist. Next moment, there was the electric swish of a score of 25-pounder shells coming in overhead. The artillery bombardment had commenced...

Scharf, standing as upright as he could, his uniform lashed about his lean frame by that fearsome wind, shrilled three blasts on his whistle. It was the signal to retreat. Already the first enemy shells were exploding to the far side of the Indians' abandoned camp. He knew what was to come. The Tommy artillery was a fearsome weapon; their gunners were well-trained and accurate – too damned accurate for him. Soon the barrage would commence creeping forward, fifty metres at a time, covering every square inch of ground. There was no time to be lost. They had to make a run for it now, while there was still a chance. Again he shrilled the signal to retreat on his whistle – three sharp blasts that cut through even the howl of that terrible wind.

Not a moment too soon. For already, Scharf, the old desert hand, was alert to the fact that the strong wind, bringing with it the cloud of flying sand, would soon be abating. Then, if the shells didn't get them, they'd be out in the open desert, with any cover long blown away by the storm, easy meat for any enemy follow-up force.

So as the wind started to slacken as he had predicted, they started to back off, the shells ploughing up great steaming holes in the sand just behind, some of them firing from the hip as they did so, as they already imagined the Indians coming out of their hiding places, ready to tackle the intruders.

Hartmann appeared out of the gloom, waving an almost empty bottle of Booth's gin. 'Them blacks like their firewater, sir,' he chortled, clearly drunk. 'Good stuff as well.'

'Shut up,' Scharf snapped angrily. 'Let's get the hell out of here—' He ducked hastily as the first shell of the new batch exploded only metres away, showering the two of them with sand.

Thus they pulled back, as the storm diminished as Scharf had predicted. The maddening, deafening howl was replaced by a soft, ever-decreasing, sad dirge. Then it was gone as they disappeared over the rise, ceased altogether, as did the artillery bombardment, leaving behind the echoing silence – and 'Crasher' Nichols, all alone (for the Indians had still not come out of their hiding places), revolver in one hand, an abandoned *Wehrmacht* tunic in the other.

Intelligence officer that he was, the ex-don had examined many an abandoned enemy tunic. But not one like this. For it did not bear the usual arm flash of the *Afrikakorps* with its customary palm tree badge. This was totally different. It was all black, with gold letters proclaiming *'BRANDENBURG'*.

Still, Nichols recognized it all right. It was the name of Admiral Canaris's house troops, the *Abwehr*'s own special regiment, something like the new-fangled SAS which was now operating in the desert under an ex-guards officer named Stirling. He frowned. Why would 'Father Christmas', as he knew the Germans called the snowy-haired, benign figure who led Germany's secret service, have his special troops attack a second-line brigade of raw Indian recruits?

THE YANKS ARE HERE

'Over there, have a care, for the Yanks are coming, over over there.'

World War One US Patriotic Song

Speedy Valley, Tunisia, January 1st 1943

'Let's be frank, gentlemen,' the cocky little American general with the craggy face said, looking around the circle of correspondents with his sharp eyes. 'I hate Jews, A-rabs, Wops, Limeys.' He gave a little pause for breath, while the American correspondents gazed at the new US Second Corps commander in amazement. 'But most of all I hate Krauts ... I hate 'em with a passion.' He spat in contempt into the dust of his 'forward outpost', as he called his new headquarters – although he was at least seventy miles behind the front. 'And that's why I'm here. I'm not here so that General Eisenhower can get on with the kikes and Limeys or the Frogs. I'm here to kill Krauts, pure and simple.' His wrinkled old face creased into a sudden engaging smile. 'But don't quote me on that, especially that bit about Ike.' He meant Eisenhower, the Supreme Commander. 'After all, Ike's a politician and gents, I'm just a plain old fighting soldier, who got kicked out of West Point twice for being so goddam dumb.'

Furiously the correspondents scribbled down his words. General Lloyd Fredendall was always good for copy. That's why the correspondents, well, at least the American ones, liked him. He certainly wasn't mealy-mouthed like most of the Allied generals new to North Africa, trying to be on their best behaviour, fearful of being sent back home before they could enjoy this war, the only one that most of them had experienced in a lifetime of service with the US Army.

The only British correspondent, Austen of the *Daily Herald* was not taken with Fredendall, who squatted down in the dust above his HQ playing the 'regular guy', as his fellow correspondents called it. He'd heard that Fredendall was an Anglophobe, like most of the US generals who had arrived with the Allied invasion force in North Africa back in the previous November. But he hadn't realized till now just how much the little American two-star general hated his allies, the 'Limeys', as he persisted in calling them.

Austen pulled a face and told himself that Fredendall's attitude didn't augur well for the near future, when the Second Corps would have to go into action against Rommel with its neighbours, the French and the British of the British First Army. Only half-listening to Fredendall's briefing, he started to jot down his own thoughts on Fredendall and his new headquarters out here in this barren wilderness on a freezing rocky height above the ancient Algerian walled city of Tebessa.

The official plan, as far as Austen had been able to ascertain, was for the Second Corps, together with the British and French fighting to the west, to soon commence a 'grand march' to the sea and split Rommel, facing Montgomery off, from the other enemy army holding the Allies in Tunisia. But on present form, Austen noted for his Labour readers back home, the US Second Corps wouldn't be moving for a long time yet. As he saw it, the cocky English-hating US general was too concerned with setting up this rear echelon HQ, and perhaps his own safety. One of Fredendall's first acts on arriving here had been to order a bulletproof Cadillac similar to Eisenhower's, and he was reported to be on the phone constantly to the port of Oran enquiring when it would arrive.

In the meantime he had three thousand troops, mostly engineers and anti-aircraft gunners, the equivalent to a whole British brigade, busy with defending his HQ and tunnelling through the rock to turn his headquarters into an underground fortification, proof against any enemy bombing or shelling. As one contemptuous US officer had told Austen on his arrival at 'Lloyd's Last Resort' (as the troops called it behind their General's back), 'With all this noise from hammering, exploding rocks and the like, Mister, you'd think we're fighting the Battle of the frigging Marne. In fact there isn't a Kraut within a dozen miles or more.'

For a while before Fredendall was ready to meet the correspondents – he'd changed from his gleaming helmet with two silver stars on it to the more folksy wool cap that made him look like some homely worker, employed perhaps in a lumber camp – Austen had inspected some of the work under the guidance of the contemptuous US officer who had snapped, 'It's like digging the frigging New York subway.' There had been large tunnels running everywhere, shored up with timber from the nearby forest, seemingly heading for the bowels of the earth. 'Every day since the General has arrived here he's been down here supervising the work, as if he's some Egyptian Pharaoh supervising the Valley of the Kings.'

Austen had grinned and wished he could have quoted the outraged US engineer officer, but he had known he couldn't. He wouldn't have gotten past the Army censors. Indeed, if his copy had come to the notice of the powers that be, he would have been winging his way back to London, probably to a job in the paper's obituary department, if the *Herald* possessed one.

So he made his own private notes and half-listened to the little US general mouthing on what he was going to do to the Krauts, once he was given his head by Eisenhower, and, Austen couldn't help thinking, finally finished his labour of love, this *great* labour of love, perhaps emulating Tebessa, that walled monument to Solomon the Eunuch and the Roman Third Legion.

'General, may I ask you one last question, sir?' the man from the *New York Times* was saying. He was dark and small, and Austen thought he might be Jewish. His tone seemed to imply it. He was respectful, but to the English correspondent, there seemed to be a note of caution in his voice as he asked what was going to be a leading question.

'Yes, sir,' Fredendall said easily. 'Fire away, but don't expect me to give any military secrets away, even to regular guys like yourselves.'

Austen could have groaned. Fredendall was playing the correspondents for all he was worth; *he* was going to have a good press from these newspapermen, who by the nature of their profession tended to be cynical.

'Well, sir,' the correspondent from the *Times* said carefully. 'The British have been stopped in Tunisia; the French, too. How, sir, do you think your Second Corps are going to do when its time comes? Have you anything special laid on for the enemy when you attack?'

In that instant, two dirty engineers passed, laden down with yet another freshly cut and trimmed tree from the local forest, obviously ready for use in one of the tunnels of 'Lloyd's Last Resort'. Wearily, they were singing the little ditty that Fredendall's staff officers had had composed for the men of the Corps. *'When the British got stuck in the mud ... and settled down for tea ... They up and beckoned for the Fighting Second in Tunisie...'*

Fredendall grinned and pointed to the two tired engineers. 'There you are, son. There's your answer,' he said triumphantly.

The *New York Times* correspondent looked puzzled. 'I don't quite understand, sir,' he commented.

Fredendall cut him short. 'Son, I'm not gonna get stuck in the mud. Nor am I gonna stop for China tea like the Limeys. I'm going to advance with my Corps hell-for-leather. The Krauts won't know what hit 'em. I'm gonna go through that Rommel and his *Afrikakorps* like shit through a goose.' Fredendall rose and tugged at the peak of his

54

woolly GI cap as if in salute. The conference was over. Like a man who had all the time in the world, Fredendall strolled away, his engineers making way for him as he entered the nearest tunnel, and the banging and hammering which had ceased for the briefing commenced again.

For a few more moments the correspondents stood around, lighting cigarettes, drinking from their silver flasks and looking undecided. 'Some general,' the man from the *Times*, who had asked the final question, said to an equally bemused Austen.

'Yes, some general,' the Englishman agreed, telling himself that Fredendall wasn't even facing Rommel in Tunisia, but the German Fifth Panzer Army, commanded by General von Arnim. Christ, if the Second Corps Leader didn't even know that, he wondered how far he'd get when the balloon finally did go up.

The *New York Times* man saw the look on the Englishman's face, and thought it not wise to continue that conversation any further. Instead he said, 'Give you a ride back to headquarters? I've got a jeep.' He named the vehicle as if it was of great importance.

Austen shook his head. 'Many thanks, but I've got my own vehicle.' He had indeed: a broken-down old utility van with a torn canvas roof and bald tyres, which he had hidden behind some rocks on the narrow winding approach road to the Second Corps HQ so that the Yanks, with their wealth of up-to-date equipment, wouldn't see it.

Thus it was as the conference broke up, and the Americans moved off swiftly to get out of the freezing wind on the heights back to their own vehicles. Austen made his own way more slowly to his battered, camouflaged van with its suspect engine, hoping that none of the Yanks spotted him as he did so. For this particular January morning, he had had enough of American superiority as far as the rest of the Allied world was concerned.

But his approach to the hidden fifteen-hundred weight Utility was not altogether unobserved. Standing there, with its engine running, a jeep was parked in the rocky path; two figures in non-descript khaki, long faded by the desert sun, were waiting in the front seats as if they had been expecting the middle-aged correspondent. For a moment, Austen's heart jumped with alarm. They could well have been members of Rommel's *Afrikakorps*, who looked and dressed like their long-time British opponents. Often the Jerries roamed far and wide behind British lines – as did the new-fangled British SAS behind theirs – hoping to pick up prisoners for interrogation. But then he spotted the difference. The two strangers in the jeep weren't wearing the typical peaked cap of the *Afrikakorps*. Indeed, one of them was wearing Arab headdress, which contrasted strangely with his tortoiseshell glasses, while the other had the maroon beret of the 11th Hussars, the 'Cherrypickers', as Austen knew the élite armoured car regiment was called in the Army, on the back of his tousled, overlong locks.

'Mr Austen,' the 'Cherrypicker' said and again the war correspondent started. How did these two strange-looking soldiers, who had appeared right out of nowhere in the middle of an American camp, miles away from the nearest British troops of General Anderson's First Army, know his name? It wasn't as if he were the correspondent for the posh London *Times* or even the *Daily Telegraph*. He was representing the working class Labour rag, the *Herald*, which ran in a state of near-permanent bankruptcy; that's why the bosses of the paper employed him. He was cheap.

'Yes,' he heard himself say, hardly recognizing his own voice.

'I wonder if you'd spare the time to come across and speak to my chief,' the 'Cherrypicker' asked very politely, and for the first time Austen noted just what a refined, 'Oxbridge' accent the soldier had for an 'other rank'.

'Why, yes,' Austen answered, wondering what he was letting himself in for. It was all very fishy. Indeed, if it hadn't been for the 'other rank' speaking Oxbridge English, he would have been very worried for his safety – and even the fact that the 'Cherrypicker' did speak like that was worrying in itself.

The man in the Arab headdress – and now Austen could see he was wearing the crown and pip of a British lieutenant-colonel – rose from his seat, touched his hand to his head in a very sloppy salute for such a high-ranking officer, and said, 'Jolly good of you to find time for me, Mr Austin. I remember reading your articles on unemployment and the Jarrow marchers when I first went up to Balliol. We were all very left-wing and Bolshy in those days, weren't we?' He beamed owlishly.

'Oh yes.' Austen was too overwhelmed by the colonel's opening words to say that a lot of people were still bolshy and left-wing even now. Nor was he flattered that this strange colonel had read his articles in the old days. 'How ... can I help you, Colonel?'

On the side of the track, the 'Cherrypicker' was brewing up in the traditional desert fashion: a two-gallon petrol can, half filled with sand and a bit of petrol thrown into it before igniting the mix and boiling water over the flickering blue flame. He turned, face red with the heat from the makeshift stove. 'Yankee tea, sir,' he said, as if Austen might want an explanation. 'Real gnat's piss. Nothing like our char. I'll make you a cup, sir.'

Again, the unlikely-looking colonel beamed at Austen owlishly through his glasses. 'I've been asked to report to General Fredendall, Mr Austen. Don't know the gentleman personally. You've just met him, and you newspaper chaps are pretty quick at assessing character. Thought you might like to give me what – er – you call the lowdown.'

Austen had never used the word 'lowdown' in the whole of his journalistic career. Still, he didn't take offence. The situation was too bizarre, and he wanted to find out more, if he could, from this strange pair who had appeared, or so it seemed, completely out of the blue. 'He's very opinionated,' he said, 'and exceedingly anti-British for a start.'

The colonel took it in his stride. 'Ex-colonialist envy, I suppose. They're still novices at this kind of fighting in Africa. We've been doing it for a couple of centuries. They'll get used to it one day when they take over. Carry on please, Mr Austen.' 'Not much else, Colonel. Just that I don't think he's up to it. Indeed, if you want a civvy's opinion, I don't think he's got a clue about what he's up against.' Austen's resentment broke through abruptly. 'He doesn't even bloody well know he's not fighting Rommel yet, instead of von Arnim. Now may I ask you a question—'

He never did get to ask his question, for the colonel with the tortoiseshells nodded in the direction of the 'Cherrypicker', who was holding up a chipped mug of steaming tea. 'Char up, Mr Austen. Better have it. We'll have to be off in half a mo. We can't keep our cousins from across the seas, as Mr Churchill calls them, waiting, can we now?'

Aachen, Germany, Jan 6th 1943

'*Leutnant Brandt zur Stelle, Herr Major*,' the young Brandenburg officer with the one arm reported. Awkwardly he lifted his left arm and saluted, as the long troop train gave off a last burst of steam like an exhausted creature after its long journey through the night from Berlin.

With a smile *Oberleutnant* Scharf returned the young officer's salute, looked at his empty right sleeve tucked neatly into his pistol belt, opened his mouth as if he were about to ask a question about how it had happened, but then changed his mind. Instead he said cheerfully, 'And where have all the ladies of the night gone here in Aachen, Brand? Remember I've just come from Africa. I haven't seen a white women for months now.' He grinned and slung his faded rucksack over his shoulder; he disdained officers who carried briefcases as 'rear echelon stallions'*, who seemed to be everywhere on the crowded platform.

Brandt returned his grin. 'Well, sir, after last night's RAF raid, they'll probably be in the shelters and cellars still, sir. There's plenty of trade there, you know. When a stubble-hopper thinks he's going to get the chop, he's either petrified or fancies dancing an urgent mattress polka before he snuffs it.'

Major Scharf's grin broadened. The young officer spoke his language, the lingo of the front swine. He liked him. 'Come on then, young man. Let's get something hot to drink. And I don't mean tea.' He shivered. It was snowing, with flakes drifting down from the bomb holes in Aachen Station's roof. But he didn't mind the snow; indeed, he enjoyed it after the burning heat of two years in the African desert. Not that the civilians and soldiers who were trudging miserably through the dirty slush did.

*German Army slang for desk officers in the rear areas of the front.

Scharf saw that there had been a great change since he had last been in the Reich. People looked wan and worn. Even the soldiers, who enjoyed a better diet than the average civilian, looked pale-faced and pinched. And everywhere there were ruins, some of them still smoking from the previous night's RAF raid. He frowned as the young, one-armed officer led him to the waiting car, which he saw, to his surprise, was no longer powered by petrol, but by a large balloon-like object, filled with gas, attached to the roof, where it wobbled and trembled in the wind like a nervous elephant. He shook his head in mock wonder and told himself that if a special élite troop such as the Brandenburgers wasn't allowed a ration of petrol, things had to be bad for the *Wehrmacht*. Aloud he said, 'Just before we wrap ourselves around a couple of glasses of strong firewater, Brandt, I'll tell you my mission there at Düren–' he meant the headquarters of the Brandenburg training battalion at the nearby Rhenish town of that name.

'Sir?' Brandt dodged the crocodile of blinded veterans in their thin blue-and-white hospital pyjamas under their greatcoats, being led through the falling snow by a group of girls in the uniform of the German Maidens, all of them singing as if they were still the vigorous young men who had once marched eastwards to defeat the Bolsheviks in those years of victory.

Scharf again refrained from comment. Indeed, he wouldn't have known what to say in the first place if he had chosen to remark about the pity of it all. 'I need bodies, Brandt. The best you have. German-Americans if you have any in training in Düren. Anyone, if you haven't, who can speak fluent American English.'

Brandt whistled softly. 'One of those ops, sir?'

Scharf nodded. 'I think so. But Field Marshal Rommel has not yet taken me into his confidence on what exactly the operation will entail.'

'I was in Chicago before the war, sir, for two years. I have an uncle there. I returned, naturally, to the Fatherland immediately we marched against Poland. So I—'

'—Can speak fluent American English.' Scharf beat him to it.

'Yessir!' Brandt actually blushed, as he added, 'I know my defect, sir. The arm, sir...' His voice faltered away to nothing. It was almost as if he was ashamed of his disability.

Scharf's heart went out to the young officer. As hard and as cynical as he had become over the years, he felt for Brandt. He guessed that a one-armed young man must feel useless and inferior in a National Social-ist culture which valued youth, physical perfection and strength so greatly. He took a chance without thinking about it and the problems his decision might cause in the future. 'Brandt, I understand your problem. But I will need an adjutant, who under-stands what we do in the Brandenburg Regi-ment and who can speak fluent American.' He saw the look of hope and joy spring into the younger man's face. 'If you'd like to give up this nice cushy "rear echelon stallion" job of yours, I'd be happy to take you—'

'Anything sir ... anything to get out of this damned garrison,' Brandt cried so eagerly that people turned and stared at him, as if he had suddenly gone crazy. Scharf pushed him hastily to the car where the driver was wait-ing, smoking fitfully and staring at the snow, which was now beginning to fall in earnest. In one and the same movement, the driver threw away his cigarette and opened the door as he said *Oberleutnant* Scharf, his face bronzed and his tunic heavy with the decora-tions and ribbons of half a dozen campaigns over three continents. 'Where to, sir?' he barked, all eager officiousness and duty now.

'Where to, my man?' Scharf echoed in great good humour. 'Where should an officer, who hasn't seen a white woman for months, if not years, want to go on his first free day in the Homeland? Why, man, to the nearest high-class knocking shop!'

Infected by the officer's high spirits and cheerful mood, the driver snapped. *'Zu Befehl, Herr Oberleutnant* ... high-class knocking shop it is, sir.' He rammed home first gear. An obscene sound like a giant wet fart, and the gas-powered car started to pull away. The new and last Rommel plan had commenced...

Obersalzburg Bavaria, Jan 6th 1943

'Meine Herren,' the giant SS flunkey in his black uniform, boots polished like mirrors, great yellow-gold lanyard swinging back and forth, bellowed at the top of his voice, as if he were back at the *Leibstandarte*'s barracks in Berlin, *'unser Führer Adolf Hitler'*.

Immediately the general officers and their chiefs-of-staff pulled at their tunics, checked if their belts and medals were sitting correctly and stiffened to attention as if they were still the raw officer-cadet recruits of decades before.

Hitler strode in purposefully, followed by his own staff and his favourite Alsatian bitch 'Blondi'. He flapped up his hand in salute, murmured *'Heil'* and said, as if he were a man in a hurry, 'Good of you to come. Please relax. We have a lot to discuss this day.'

They did so, all but Rommel. In the old

days he had always been in the forefront of such gatherings of top soldiers. Now, with his reputation in abeyance, Hitler's staff had left him to the rear, where he could stare out of the picture window at the snow, falling on the township of Berchtesgaden below in a solid white sheet, blotting out the place. It was a sombre winter vista, which matched his mood.

Next to Hitler, his chief-of-staff Field Marshal Keitel, tall, wooden-necked, pompous and stupid, raised his bejewelled marshal's staff and said, 'It concerns the situation in Africa, *mein Führer*, may we commence?'

He spoke so loudly that Blondi fled in panic into a corner, where she began to urinate over the boot of the SS officer posted there. The man dared not look down or move. The Alsatian continued to urinate till his boot was dripping with pee. No one seemed to notice.

'Please,' Hitler said in an unusually sombre voice. In better days, Rommel remembered, the Führer had always spoken at the top of his voice when he addressed his senior military commanders. Then, he had often wondered whether he was still reliving his days as a humble corporal in the Imperial Army, when it was customary for other ranks to bellow when addressing an officer. 'Please, may I say from the outset of this

66

conference, gentlemen, that I and Germany cannot afford another Stalingrad. The army in Africa must remain intact to give my people their confidence back in their soldiers. We cannot lose a whole army of German soldiers such as Paulus' – for a moment his face was contorted in contempt at the mention of the German Field Marshal, who had surrendered his Sixth Army to the Russians – 'has just done. So, with that in mind, please start, gentlemen.'

Keitel nodded to von Arnim, who was as stiff-backed and wooden as Keitel. Rommel frowned. Obviously the general, who commanded the Fifth Panzer Army and who had stopped the Anglo-French advance in Tunisia the previous month, was now in favour. He, the one-time Hitler favourite, who had failed to stop Montgomery advancing from Egypt after the Battle of El Alamein so that the Tommies were now poised on the Libyan-Tunisian border on the Mareth Line, was no longer the 'Führer's darling', as his envious fellow generals had once described him and his victorious *Afrikakorps*. He sighed, and continued to look miserably at the falling snow.

Von Arnim wasted no time. *'Mein Führer,* we have held the enemy in Tunisia with an army which is far outnumbered by the Western Allies. Twice we have tried to capitalize on that victory by attacking through the two passes that lead into Western Tunisia, one held by the British, the other by the Americans. Although both of the defending enemy groups suffered grievous losses at our hands and will undoubtedly not be in a position to attack till the spring and better weather, we were unable to break through.' He paused and let Hitler digest his words for a few moments before adding, 'We simply didn't have the resources in men and armour.'

For a moment Hitler frowned at von Arnim's mention of his lack of resources, but then he gave a weak smile and said, 'You did well, General.'

Von Arnim turned and looked pointedly at a gloomy Rommel, whom he didn't like.

It was then that Hitler turned and strode over to the large map of North Africa, marked 'SECRET' in red letters, which had appeared miraculously from the ceiling and now covered most of the wall opposite. The soft whirr of the hidden electric motor seemed to alert Blondi that her master was moving. She shook herself and padded over to where he now stood, leaving the giant SS officer still standing motionless in a steaming puddle of dark brown urine. Under other circumstances, Rommel might have smirked to himself at the SS flunkey's discomfiture. But not now. Soon, he knew, he'd be taken to task by Hitler. He waited, gathering his thoughts for what he realized would have to be his defence of his own lack of success and initiative.

Hitler was obviously well-briefed, as always. 'At the moment, gentlemen,' he started in straightaway, 'the greatest danger to both the *Afrikakorps* and the Fifth Panzer Army is the US Second Corps, with some thirty thousand men, and other American troops in the Tebessa area.' He tapped the map without even looking to check if he had hit the right spot – he had. 'If this American force, which includes one armoured division, breaks out from Gafsa towards Gabes – here – it will be able to split your two armies.' Hitler sighed a little, like a man sorely tried. 'And I don't need to tell you, gentlemen, what that will mean for German armies in North Africa. In essence, therefore, gentlemen, if we are to survive in Tunisia, we must break up the American assembly area in the south west around Tebessa.'

He paused to let his words sink in before turning his attention on Rommel for the first time since the conference had commenced. 'The Englishman, Montgomery, as we know, is proceeding at such a leisurely pace against the *Afrikakorps* that I think we can safely say that the *Afrikakorps* might well have at least two weeks to carry out any mischief we may plan in that part of the world while the rear-guard holds the door at Mareth – here. Why,' his voice rose encouragingly, 'we might even plan a little local surprise attack on the Mareth Line which could keep Montgomery from starting his great push westwards for even longer, say one whole month – and a lot of things can happen in a month, gentlemen, as you well know.'

There was a murmur of agreement from the other officers. Not from Rommel. He couldn't contain his growing anger any longer. These toadies were living in cloud-cuckoo land. They hadn't the foggiest idea of what was really going on in North Africa. *'Mein Führer,'* he said, keeping his voice low, though his hands trembled with rage. 'There can be no talk of a spoiling attack. I have already done a reconnaissance of the whole of the Mareth Line. Even at its weakest point, where it was held by untrained black levées from India, it withstood our efforts. The same cannot be said for our own 'door', as you have called it. We are holding the Tommies with a handful of German soldiers and some ninety thousand Italians, and we all know the Italians' value as soldiers. They're interested in wine, women and song, not war. Their commanders are silly fops, their equipment totally out of date. Why, even the Tommies will not use Italian grenades, in case they blow off the grenade thrower's hand. If Montgomery attacks, he will go through my Italians – and he knows where they are located – within twenty-four hours.'

There was a shocked silence at Rommel's outburst. His yellow, emaciated face suddenly flushed with so much talking, Rommel faced them defiantly. He had never been one to pull his punches; why should he do so now, he told himself, when his star was on the wane and he was out of favour with the dictator who had once hung on his every word?

Even Hitler was caught off guard by Rommel's passionate outburst, so much so that his foot twitched and struck Blondi. Immediately the Alsatian bitch, sensitive to her master's every mood, slipped away and headed for the long-suffering SS officer standing still in his puddle of smelly urine.

But Rommel was not finished yet. He had known Hitler too long. He knew the Führer loved to surround himself with *optimistic* lackeys. Hitler hated pessimists and bad news. Personally, Rommel felt there was no hope for the German troops in Africa. Already he had bought a English-German dictionary and was practising English, just in case he was trapped in the Dark Continent and had to go into Anglo-American captivity. Naturally, he was going to keep his total disbelief in any chance of a change of future there to himself. Instead he said, 'I have spoken my mind, *mein Führer*. I am sure I speak for General von Arnim as well when I say that unless we are substantially reinforced in North Africa there is little chance of a real victory there.'

Von Arnim threw him a glance of sheer hatred, but then consoled himself with the thought that Rommel had told the truth, not he. Now, when the final crunch came, he couldn't be marked as a defeatist by the Führer. Rommel would bear that responsibility for having stated his misgivings in front of the Führer and the assembled generals. He waited for the one-time ever-victorious 'Desert Fox' to dig himself ever deeper into the shit. He was in for a surprise.

For now Rommel continued. 'But so saying, I am prepared to do something – *anything* – I can with those limited resources, *mein Führer*.'

Hitler's anger vanished immediately. He knew full well from the past how often Rommel, once his favourite commander, had managed to drag victory out of apparent defeat at the very last moment. 'Please carry on, Field Marshal,' he said.

'Well, I have already prepared a small special force – its details need not concern us here. It will suffice to say that it is being organized at this very moment here in the Reich. This force will, within the week, be testing the enemy defences in south-west Tunisia for weak spots. Once they are discovered, my Tenth Panzer Division, which is up to strength, has already been alerted to be on twenty-four hours notice to attack. The—'

'*Attack, Rommel*!' The rest of the Desert Fox's words were drowned by Hitler's excited cry.

'Attack, *mein Führer* ... Yes, that is what I said.'

Hitler was abruptly transformed. The scowl left his face as if by magic. He advanced on a now coldly smiling, superior Rommel. He had achieved what he had come here to do. Naturally, he didn't believe for one second that any attack in Tunisia would succeed. But Hitler wanted his damned fool attack with the miserable resources available in North Africa; he should have it. It would only postpone the tragedy to come. Hitler, for his part, advanced on the haggard field marshal, barging through his excited generals, ignoring von Arnim totally. Arms extended in that old florid Austrian gesture of his, he took Rommel's hands and cried, 'Rommel, what a military genius you are! Once again you'll pull the chestnuts out of the fire for me. I thank you from the bottom of my heart.'

In the corner Blondi responded to her master's changed mood by wagging her tail vigorously. The SS officer whose boot still dripped cursed the piss-assed bitch. Under his breath, naturally. He didn't want to be sent to a concentration camp. These days, a nervous Führer was only too quick to send any one of his household who offended him to one of the death camps, even SS officers.

Thus, while they talked excitedly on the top of the mountain, sheltered from the blinding snow, Rommel told himself they were like passengers in some latter-day *Titanic*, doomed even in this moment of supposed triumph...

Düren, Jan 8th 1943

Oberleutnant Scharf, still baggy-eyed from his night in the Aachen officers' brothel, did not particularly like what he saw in the battered Brandenburg barracks in Düren. Perhaps it was the fact that, like Aachen, Düren had been hit again by the enemy bombers, not only those of the RAF at night, but during daylight on the previous day when, high, high in the winter sky, the *Amis* came in from over Belgium and, with apparent majestic ease, had unloaded several tons of high explosive on the little Rhenish town, untroubled by the place's anti-aircraft fire, which couldn't reach them at their height.

Even in the time he had been away in Africa, Germany appeared to have been changed totally. Everywhere there were the same old slogans promising victory – *'DIE RADER ROLLEN FUR DEN KRIEG'*, *'SIEG ODER TOT'** and the like, but the heart seemed have gone from the people. Even when a military band paraded through the wintry streets, all rattling kettledrums and blaring bombastic brass, the people's spirits were not uplifted, and little boys in the uniform of the youth movements no longer marched with wooden rifles over their shoulders, proudly in step with the bandsmen.

Nor was Scharf too pleased with the recruits that Brandt had paraded before him the previous day for his inspection and approval. Admittedly most of them were German-Americans of one sort or another, who had lived in the German sections of New York or worked in the Milwaukee breweries; there was even one named Schroeder who came from a pure German-speaking community in rural Texas. Yet there was something more of the American than German, he thought, in their make-up. They were too

---

**Wheels Roll For Victory, Victory Or Death.*

75

'relaxed', as they liked to say. They lounged, showed little eagerness, and some even chewed gum, and it seemed to Scharf that most of them had returned to the Fatherland not on account of any sense of duty, but more to escape the Great Depression and joblessness which had plagued America until 1941, when she had gone to war and industry had begun to flourish once more.

He recalled the survivors of that abortive reconnaissance on the Mareth Line, still presumably on leave in Tunis under the command of ex-legionnaire Hartmann, the born survivor. They were a different breed from these new recruits. The Hartmann group might well be adventurers, 'old hares' who displayed the veterans' contempt for great causes and ideologies. Yet when it came to action, the Hartmann bunch could be relied upon to put their hearts into it, to risk their lives if necessary, even if it was only for a pack of *Ami* Chesterfields or a Hershey bar of over-sweet chocolate.

There was one soldier among the new recruits in particular whom he took an instant dislike to. He bore the very English name of Jenkins, and not a German one, however corrupted over the years in America, as did the others. He was tall and rangy, his dark eyes set in a permanent look of what they called in the *Wehrmacht* 'dumb insolence'. It was a term that described a soldier's attitude more than what he did and said. In Jenkins's case, it seemed that it took him a great effort to come to the position of attention when addressing an officer or senior NCO. Indeed, so far Scharf hadn't seen him salute either rank. But he had seen the German-American spit contemptuously on the ground of the square after being reprimanded by the battalion's sergeant-major. In itself that was a punishable offence. But Scharf had let it go. He reasoned that these German-Americans had picked up too many *Ami* habits during their long years in that far country, and he didn't have the time to knock them out of these 'volunteers', if they were really volunteers.

After that first inspection of these new Brandenburgers that he would be taking to Africa soon, Scharf asked the eager young one-armed officer, *Leutnant* Brandt, what he thought and knew of Jenkins. 'Not much, sir,' Brandt had to confess.

'He didn't come to us through the usual route.' He meant via the Party's National Socialist Overseas Service. 'He came from the front.'

'The front?' Scharf exclaimed, surprised.

'Yessir. He'd been awarded the Iron Cross, First Class, there in Russia.'

'But he's not wearing decoration,' Scharf

had objected.

'No sir. He wasn't allowed to, sir. He was in disgrace, you see.' He frowned. 'You see, he won it taking out a Russki strongpoint, and then he was supposed to bring the Russian commander, a general indeed, and his staff for interrogation. Apparently, as I've heard the story, they had vital information that Intelligence wanted desperately. Normally no one would have given a damn what happened to Ivan prisoners. You know what the east front's like, sir. Not exactly a finishing school for refined high-born ladies.'

He didn't smile at his own attempt at humour. Neither did Scharf. He was too curious about what Jenkins had done. 'And?' he queried swiftly.

Brandt gave a little shrug of his skinny shoulders. 'He shot the lot of them in cold blood. No apparent reason.' He shrugged again. 'Just like that. Anyway, that's the reason for his landing up here in Düren. The powers that be want him out of the Reich as soon as possible. This seemed the ideal possibility of doing so, *Oberleutnant*. After all, he speaks fluent American and at the same time he's had combat experience, even winning a decoration for bravery in the face of the enemy.'

Scharf laughed a little cynically. 'Oh yes, the very best type. Field Marshal Rommel will be overjoyed to number Private Jenkins among the ranks of the *Afrikakorps*, eh?'

Brandt was too young still, despite his terrible wound, to have become cynical like Scharf yet. His face earnest, he replied, 'Well, sir, the others are good quality human material, sir, and sir, remember that Field Marshal Rommel also uses penal battalions in Africa.'*

'Yes, to pick up mines without mine detectors and attack fortified positions without high explosives or machine guns.

He soon deals with that particular problem. I doubt that many of the men in *his* penal battalions ever return to a grateful Fatherland with their crimes atoned for.' He saw the look on Brandt's face and clapped him on the shoulder. 'Now don't take it all as serious as beer, young man. With the two of us in charge, I think we'll be able to cope even with Private Jenkins. Now let's wrap ourselves around a nice hot glass of strong tea and punch. After Africa, I'm beginning to feel this shitty cold.' He shivered dramatically and started in the direction of the *Offizierskasino*.

Behind them, lounging lazily against the side of a winter-skeletal tree as usual, Jenkins glowered at the back of the two officers.

*Formed of military criminals.

'Frigging officers and gents,' he cursed to himself in English. 'I've shat the bastards.' He hawked and spat into the dirty snow, as to the west the village sirens in the Hurtgen Forest started to sound their dire warning. The *Ami* bombers were coming back yet again.

Kronprinz Hotel, Berchtesgaden, Jan 8th 1943

'Our fate is gradually being decided, my dear Lu,' Rommel wrote in his careful, precise hand, considering every word as a good general should. Outside, the snow had ceased. Now the mountains circling the little Bavarian town sparkled in the new snow. Sledges pulled by farmhorses slid along the streets, bells tinkling. A company of mountain troops from their barracks in nearby Bad Reichenhall marched out to some new exercise singing lustily about their 'nut-brown maiden'.

It was a happy picture, filled with hope and the beauty of nature, undisturbed by the terrible war raging through the rest of Europe. Once upon a time, when Rommel had himself been one of those *'Jäger'*, had fought against the Italians in the high mountains not far from where he wrote now, his heart would have leapt at the sight of so much pristine-pure peaceful beauty. Not

80

now; his mind was too full of what awaited him now. Why the Führer had forbidden him to spend as much as a day with his beloved wife Lu and his young son, who might well be a soldier himself soon; the boy was patriotic and eager enough.

With heavy heart, the sick field marshal, once the admiration of friend and foe alike – why, hadn't even that drunkard Churchill praised him indirectly in the English parliament? – took up his pen once again ... 'I must confess to you, darling, that it would need a miracle for us to hold out much longer in Africa ... But I must do my duty, as I have always done, as you well know ... What happens now will be in God's hands. But we will go on fighting as long as it is at all possible.' Wearily, he laid down the pen; he hadn't the concentration to continue and write to his wife of so many good and happy years any more. Besides, he had said enough as it was. If his letter fell into the wrong hands, he might well be accused of defeatism, and he knew what that meant. Hitler was already shooting generals who failed him. Not that he feared death. But his wife and son might suffer, too, and he wouldn't have been able to tolerate that. The letter would have to be carried by hand by one of his trusted officers to his home in Swabia.

He forgot his personal problems for a moment, and concentrated again on the new plan which had occupied his mind ever since the sixth of January, when he had achieved that minor victory at the Führer's conference and put von Arnim's nose out for a while.

Already one of his best armoured divisions had been transferred to the latter's Fifth Panzer Army. More would follow. In the end, they'd even take his Italian armour off him, for what it was worth. He, the Desert Fox, who had once been Germany's most celebrated tank commander, would be left with a handful of German and Italian infantry to fight to the last or face the ignominy of surrender – and he would rather shoot himself than do that. He was not going to be a second Field Marshal von Paulus, who had surrendered with his Sixth Army at Stalingrad. German field marshals didn't surrender. They took the 'officer's way out' and shot themselves.

Perhaps, in the end, Hitler would save him from that final disgrace and fly him out of Africa while there was still time. After all, everyone knew that he was a sick man, who had survived the diseases and privations of the dark continent much longer than any of his original staff, although they had been much younger than he was. His staff had all been killed or invalided back to the Reich long before. He was the sole survivor of the *Afrikakorps*'s original staff.

But before the inevitable happened, whatever form it might take, he knew he needed a victory, although it wouldn't be a lasting one. But how could he pull it off with fifteen thousand Germans, mostly infantry, fifteen thousand Italians, and one sole under-strength panzer division, the Tenth?

Naturally, he would hit the *Amis*, as he had already told the Führer he would. They were the enemy's freshest troops in North Africa and they were well equipped, too. He knew from Intelligence that their morale was good. However, in the brief skirmishes that had taken place between them and von Arnim's troops, they had shown they possessed little battle experience, and that they were badly led. The rank and file had surrendered easily, and in one case their tankers had fired upon their own infantry in panic. Captured British and French soldiers had reported they called the Yankees 'our Italians'.

As he sat there in the loneliness of the big, panelled Bavarian hotel room, listening to the tinkle of sledge-bells outside, the screams and laughter of the home-coming school children snow-balling one another, he told himself he could no longer achieve even a small-scale victory against Montgomery's seasoned troops. But he could against the ill-led green innocents of the US Second Corps.

He rose ponderously and walked slowly over to the big map of North Africa spread across the table next to the green-tiled oven which heated the place and crackled merrily with the wooden logs cut in the nearby forests. He stared down at it with his old trained skill.

The terrain through which he would attack was difficult – parched sand plains in part, but mostly hilly with few passes that were suitable for armour. He had some information about those passes through the hills, but he doubted if it was totally accurate. Besides, what if the *Amis* had dug in some good quality troops? A few steadfast infantry, armed with anti-tank guns and able to call up air support swiftly would speedily dash any hope of thrusting through an armoured division in double-quick time.

He pondered the matter for much longer than he usually took to make a strategic decision and he knew it. But he could not afford to make a mistake now, and his brain wasn't as good as it had once been. Finally he told himself, 'I need a detailed reconnaissance of one of those passes, and a recce by some force that will ensure that any defending force there will be eradicated speedily.

Nothing must hold up a quick advance and a decisive blow.'

He nodded his head as if agreeing with himself, and walked to the window. For a moment or two he gazed down at the school kids throwing snowballs with their mothers, feathered hats waving in the breeze, shouting for them to hurry on home. He remembered how he had once been like those same kids, happy, carefree, concerned only with the simple pleasures of childhood. What would become of those children if Germany lost the war and the Fatherland was occupied by the enemy, especially by the Ivans? How long would they survive in the hands of that half-wild people, thirsting for their savage revenge for what the Germans had done to them and their country? No, come what may, he had to do what he could to stave off the inevitable for as long as possible.

Filled with new resolve, he returned to his writing pad and added a last few lines before he returned to North Africa and the final act of the drama that awaited him there. 'Darling Lu, pray for Germany ... pray for me, your loving husband.' But even as he wrote, his gaze fell yet again on the big map of North Africa next to the green-tiled stove and the name of the place where he knew it must happen. Now it came to Rommel with the instant recognition of a vision, one that needed no explanation or analysis. It was there that he would beat the Americans and achieve his last victory in Africa. The name was Kasserine ... the pass at Kasserine, it would be there that he would teach the strangers from across the sea that they would be punished for their insolent and un- necessary interference in the affairs of Old Europe. *Kasserine...*

The Station, Niederprum, Jan 8th–9th 1943

The American daylight bombers had hardly vanished that short snowy January day when the sirens had began to sound all over the Eifel border area below Düren. The RAF was on its way. In full force. This, it seemed, was to be a repetition of the great English thousand-bomber raid on Cologne the pre- vious spring.

Their squadrons of Halifax and Lancaster four-engined bombers swooped out of the sky all along the German frontier with Occupied Belgium and Luxembourg, from Aachen to Trier on the River Moselle.

Ignoring the searchlights and massed defensive fire of the flak batteries protecting the strategic railway line that ran from Cologne down to Aachen and then along the Reich's frontier, the English 'terror fliers' were obviously coming in for the kill. They knew the bad weather over Germany made it difficult for *Luftwaffe* HQ to scramble its fighters at Wahn and Buechel in time to stop them before they headed back over Belgium, using the shortest route to reach their damned homeland to dine off those greasy eggs and salty bacon, which apparently was regarded as a great culinary treat in that country.

Everywhere as the enemy bombers completed their deadly work and fled for home, the alarms sounded at barracks, fire-stations, civil defence posts throughout the Eifel. Villages, and in particular railway stations, had been hit everywhere. As the phones jingled, the teleprinters clattered and the sirens of the ambulances and fire-trucks shrilled their urgent warnings, it seemed as if the whole area was aflame or already in ruins. Everywhere, hospitals and first aid stations were already packed with the wounded and burnt. Casualties were already being shipped across the frontier to the German-speaking parts of Luxembourg and the Belgian East Cantons.

Still there was not enough help to go round, especially where civilians were trapped in the still-smoking ruins, with the threat of unexploded or delayed-fuse bombs about to explode and kill them at any moment. It was thus that at the command of the local military district governor, a full general himself, the Brandenburgers, despite being a special unit on twenty-four-hour alert for dispatch overseas, were ordered to form small rescue teams immediately. Using all available transport (even at the expense of their meagre, precious petrol ration), they were to spread out along the railway line between Düren and nearby Monchau, and commence rescue operations at once. In particular, a large team was urgently needed just outside the picturesque pre-war tourist town of Monschau. Here, a large training school for Hitler Maiden leaders had been hit. Some fifty girls between sixteen and eighteen had been trapped there, and there was the danger that a landmine dropped in the local stream might explode at any moment. Time was of the essence.

Oberleutnant Scharf had not liked the general's order one bit. He told himself he couldn't waste men, especially when they were needed so urgently in Africa. As he told Brandt, busy organizing his German-Americans into a single large team, 'I suppose I could appeal to Field Marshal Rommel to have the order rescinded. But this is what we're fighting for – the safety of our own civilians. Therefore, we go.'

They had. They had driven from the Düren barracks with their lights full on, no longer blacked out, down the winding country roads towards the Belgian frontier, and then on down from the hills into the great, long serpentine road that led to the beautiful tourist town down in the valley below, which had been a favourite spot for honeymooners before the war. But there was no longer anything beautiful about Monschau this grey winter dawn.

Smoke plumes, tinged a cherry-red with still-burning fires, were rising everywhere from the bombed half-timbered houses of the place. Huge smoking craters, looking like the work of giant moles, were blocking the cobbled medieval streets, as fire-crews and frantic civilians tried to get through to the trapped locals.

Outside the hospital, marked with a huge red cross on its slate roof, but still bombed, corpses sprawled everywhere as walking patients had attempted to flee the wards, only to run right into the bombs. Now bits and pieces of bloody bodies hung from the skeletal trees like macabre human fruit, dripping blood and gore.

Behind an awe-stricken, horrified Scharf, who in his time had seen so much carnage but nothing like this terrible scene, Jenkins, the tough German-American, breathed, 'Holy strawsack, what a place to loot ... Holy shit and shingle, look at that jeweller's shop, it's wide open.'

Scharf dropped his hand to his pistol holster, suddenly ablaze with rage. 'Another remark like that from you, you callous swine, and I'll shoot you on the damned spot!'

Five minutes later all of them, officer and simple soldier, were toiling with their primitive entrenching tools, intended for digging an infantryman's slit trench, and picks borrowed from the local agricultural college, working all-out trying to clear the rubble from the girls trapped in the cellars below, while the corpses already excavated were draped in long lines outside on the water-soaked cobbles with sobbing local women covering their wrecked young bodies with blankets and old potato sacks.

Two hours later, the police with their Alsatian sniffer dogs arrived from Euskirchen and let the animals loose in order to find out where the main groups of the girls were trapped – if they were still alive – in the cellars below. The dogs struck lucky. Even as they started to scratch at the smoking rubble with their paws, the sweating Brandenburgers leaning on their shovels or taking long draughts from their water-bottles, while the women sobbed and sobbed, trying to stifle their tears by throwing their aprons across their ashen faces, the listeners could hear the first faint knocking from below.

Scharf turned excitedly to Brandt. 'There's

some smart girl down there, Brandt. She's knocking on some sort of hollow pipe, perhaps the major water one. It's giving a greater degree of resonance and she must know it. That's why we can hear the knocking. All right,' he raised his voice and yelled to the fat, middle-aged cop in charge of the Alsatians, 'call 'em off for the moment, *Herr Kommissar*. We've got 'em.'

Now they proceeded to clear away the smoking rubble, very carefully. In some cases they moved the smashed masonry and charred beams by hand, while the one-armed *Leutnant* Brandt listened tautly, head cocked to one side for the first sound of voices from below, or any unusual rumbling that might indicate the lower floor was about to collapse and bury the trapped girls for ever.

Fortunately, that didn't happen. In the end, the hollow, magnified tapping from below ceased. It was replaced by a high-pitched, slightly hysterical girl's voice calling, 'We're all right ... To the left of where you're digging now ... Be careful please ... the walls down here are making a funny creaking noise ... But please comrades – *hurry*!'

It was just then that Jenkins made what was, for him, a strange, if not decidedly unusual offer. 'There's a narrow shaft over here, *Oberleutnant*,' he called to Scharf as they commenced digging and burrowing once more. 'I'm thin enough to get down it. With your permission, sir, I'll have a go at trying to get down it and see what I can find ... Perhaps I can help to direct the digging from down there, sir.'

It was a suggestion that surprised Scharf. But at this moment of crisis, with the possibility of the cellar below collapsing, it was one he couldn't refuse, though he didn't trust the hard-faced killer as far as he could throw him. 'Yes,' he called back, 'get to it. Take a rope down with you. Might come in useful. *Los!*'

'Sir.' Jenkins was all urgent eagerness. 'I'm off now, sir.' He grabbed a rope, and while Scharf paused to watch him, face heavy with doubt, the German-American slithered into the hole and was gone almost immediately, trailing the stout rope behind him.

But in the end, it seemed they didn't need Jenkins's services. Some ten or fifteen minutes later, working all-out, the Brandenburgers had cleared a hole in the roof of the cellar, which had obviously been used as an air-raid shelter, though the stout timbers reinforcing its walls had snapped off like matchsticks under the bomb blast, and the first dirty girlish faces looked up at them from below. Five minutes after that, passing down their water-bottles, and in one case a bottle of brandy for those who might need it to revive them, the first of the Brandenburgers, led by Scharf personally, were lowering themselves carefully into the dark, dust-filled interior of the cellar, which still gave off the acrid, biting smell of high explosive.

All at once, the rescuers were surrounded by excited girls, caked in dust, skinny legs naked save for the standard black knickers of the 'German Maiden' organization. They clustered about the Brandenburgers, grasping and kissing their hands in gratitude. Some even flung their arms around the soldiers and hugged the embarrassed men, crying over and over again in broken voices, 'We're saved ... Thank God, we're saved!'

Scharf stepped into the background while his men enjoyed the satisfaction of knowing that they had saved the girls and savoured, he supposed, the youthful charms they had to offer, though he told himself there wasn't much of a real women about their pubescent bodies. He had given himself a grim, lone task. With Jenkins's help, wherever he was at this moment, he would have the dead kids hauled up to the surface by means of the German-American's rope and covered up like the rest of their dead before the survivors were brought up.

Clicking on the *Wehrmacht* torch attached to his tunic, he started to thread his way through the ruins, dodging the smashed timbers, his gaze fixed carefully on the rubble everywhere for the first sight of some unfortunate's dead body.

But it wasn't a dead body that he encountered. It was, instead, the missing Jenkins, pinned in the circle of bright light at the end of the dust-filled corridor, facing a girl who stared back at him defiantly, her hands clenched to her sides defensively, her naked breasts revealed in all their beauty.

Scharf took in the situation immediately. Nothing had happened as yet. But he did not need a crystal ball to realize that if he hadn't appeared, something very wrong would have occurred in the next few minutes. His free hand dropped to his pistol and he ordered, trying to control his rising temper, 'Get about your business, Jenkins. They need you inside there to get the girls out. Off you go – double-quick time.'

Jenkins shot him a look of absolute, naked hate. For a moment he hesitated. But even in that poor light, he could see how Scharf's knuckles whitened on the butt of his pistol. Whatever he had in mind at that moment – and Scharf guessed it could only be something evil – he changed. Tamely, head bowed so that the officer couldn't see the fury in his features, he brushed by Scharf and disappeared down the corridor.

Despite the fact that she had just escaped being raped and that she was clad only in the black knickers of her movement, though these, unconventionally, were made of silk, not cotton, the girl, who might have been seventeen or eighteen, remained calm. 'Thank you,' she said simply, not attempting to cover her breasts, which were full and mature like those of an older woman. 'I am very grateful to you, *Oberleutnant.*'

Scharf told himself she wasn't from the Rhineland. Her voice was that of Northern Germany with the pure accent of Westphalia, perhaps the Hanover region. Nor did she have the reddened hands of the local girls, used to hard work on their poor, scruffy farms. This was an educated girl, he guessed, of good family. Perhaps she was a *Führerin*, a leader, as many of them were, despite the Party's claim that in the new National Socialist state everyone was equal.

Next moment the girl made it clear she was what he thought she was. She gave a slight bow from the waist and said, 'May I introduce myself? Irma von Klarfeld, *Bannführerin, Mittelmosel.*'*

He touched his hand to his dust-covered cap in acknowledgement. *'Angenehm.'* He forced himself to take his gaze away from the

* *Group Leader, Central Moselle District.*

girl's splendid breasts. 'We must get you something to cover your—'

'Breasts.' She completed the sentence for him without the slightest hesitation.

'Yes,' he lowered his gaze, wondering if she had seen him ogling her.

If she had, she made nothing of it. There was nothing of the youthful temptress about her. Indeed, she was direct and purposeful, almost like a man. She said, 'My girls – are they all right, *Oberleutnant*?'

'Yes, well, those in the cellar are.' He bit his bottom lip momentarily. 'I'm afraid, however, that there may have been casualties among the others.'

'The casualties of war. The price of victory, eh, *Herr Oberleutnant*.' There was no mistaking the bitter cynicism in her voice now. It was the tone, not of a young girl, but that of a mature woman who had seen much of the world and its evil ways.

He didn't reply, as she stared at him, a look of almost accusation on her pretty dark face, and for once he was glad at that moment that the sirens had commenced their dread wail once again and obviated any need to answer that unspoken question. Instead he heard himself say, 'Let's get back. The *Amis* are on their way again. Round up your girls. *Dalli ... dalli*!'

They became lovers that very same night:

the seventeen-year-old BIM leader and *Oberleutnant* Scharf, already in his twenties. Almost immediately after the sirens had signalled the return of the American Flying Fortresses, he had rushed the girls out of that particular cellar into one of the bomb-proof caves beneath the hills that surround-ed Monschau – the terrified youngsters had refused to stay in the cellar which had already been bombed. For his part, he had taken a room in one of the former hotels for honeymooners, *'Hotel zum Weissen Schwan,'* now not at all white and swan-like, but grey and delapidated. But at least the virtually deserted building, worn by the years of the war and few customers save servicemen and their Belgian whores, did serve a hot, un-rationed meal; and Scharf had decided, before he returned to the monotonous tinned fare of 'Old Man', reputedly made from the flesh of old men from Berlin's workhouses, in the desert, that he was going to have one last decent German meal, complete with fresh meat. To his surprise, Irma von Klarfeld had insisted that she be quartered in the same shabby hotel. As she explained, 'My girls are locals from the peasantry. They're happy without me when off duty. They can eat the way they want,' she laughed, a surprisingly light laugh for so tough a young woman, 'pick their noses with their forks if they wish. Let them have their peace away from my supposed eagle North German eye.'

But Scharf was not fated to eat his fresh meat that last night in Germany. The 'terror fliers' of the English air force saw to that. Hardly had they sat down in the dingy little *stube* of the inn, decorated with dusty antlers killed in the local forests by some long-dead hunters, the only light cast by the inn-keeper's flickering petroleum lanterns, when the sirens sounded yet again and the wireless station tuned to *Luftwaffe* HQ announced its usual warning, 'English bombers flying from the direction of Eupen in the East Cantons heading in the German Eifel. All places between St Vith and Bitburg are warned—' Even before the warning had ceased, the bombs were thudding down between Malmedy and Monschau, and the terrified innkeeper was urging them to go down to yet another cellar.

The German Maiden refused stubbornly. 'If I'm going to die, I want to die in comfort and above ground,' and Scharf, the survivor of many a savage battle over these last ter-rible years of total war, had no other option but to do the same.

In his candle-lit bedroom with the walls heaving from the first of the bombs dropping in the hills above Monschau, he took her in his arms and kissed her fiercely, almost brutally. She responded wildly, with an abandon that he had not expected from such a cold North German type. She pressed herself against him. He felt those delightful breasts up against his naked chest; her soft rounded stomach thrust against the hardness of his loins. She gasped crazily, as if she were running a great race. Together, clinging to one another, they fell on the ancient, creaking inn bed, the room's only decoration save for a rickety chair and the customary crucifix above the marble.

Her eager tongue burrowed deep into his gaping mouth, wet with saliva. His hand felt up her stocking. It stopped at her black, silky knickers. 'Go on,' she breathed fervently. 'For God's sake, don't stop now!'

'But you're only a kid—'

He never finished. She grabbed his hand hard and forced it beneath the silk. He hesitated no longer. His greedy, striving fingers found the warm, wet softness. Suddenly the difference in their ages, the bombs, the war, were forgotten. Now there was only one thing of importance. It overshadowed everything else.

Once, a bomb landed close by. The whole inn shook. Flakes of plaster came raining down from the ancient ceiling. They did not even notice. They were too wrapped in their all-consuming passion as they writhed back and forth on the squeaking, protesting wooden bed. Their shadows, gigantically magnified by the flickering petroleum lantern, continued their frantic dance. For their fevered desire consumed them, as they loved one another as if there had never ever been such a love-making in the whole history of the world...

But the war-torn world outside could not be forgotten altogether. As the sirens sounded the 'all clear', echoing and re-echoing around the surrounding hills, she asked, suddenly calm and quiet, 'Why?'

'Why what?'

'You know,' she said, 'Continue fighting like this. Tomorrow you leave. The day after, you may be dead. Why do it?'

He tried to joke. 'They'll shoot me if I don't go, Irma.'

'But we can't win. You know it; they know it. The English and the *Amis* will win in the end. See what they've already done to your Homeland.'

'Probably. But we must fight on.' He stared up at the ceiling, as outside the ambulances raced up the Serpentine, their sirens and bells shrieking urgently.

'But why?' she persisted. She leaned forward on one elbow, her hair dangling down, the nipple of her naked breast almost touching his face.

'Because, my dear Irma, there is nothing else left for me and my kind to do but fight. That's all we know now. It's all we've done for years. What else is there but battle for the likes of us?' He shrugged, and taking his gaze from the ceiling, looked at her. 'But war.'

She was silent for what seemed a long time. Scharf didn't want to talk any more. There was no purpose to it, he knew. They were men doomed, with the mark of Cain carved on their foreheads. There was no future for them. He reached up and attempted to take her nipple in his mouth. She shook her head impatiently and drew back.

'Do you know what my girls and I talk about on the days like these when we spend most of our time in the cellars?'

'Food?' he ventured.

She shook her head.

'Boys?' he tried with a half-smile on his lips, not wanting to be drawn into any more serious discussion. 'Handsome boys in uniform with chestfuls of medals?'

She looked at him sternly and his smile vanished. 'No, we talk about death – and what we will do when it's over and we've lost the war ... and the enemy takes his revenge for what we have done to him.' She bit her bottom lip, and abruptly he realized just how frightened she really was under that North

German exterior of hers. 'Some of the girls say they'll take poison, but where in three devils would they get poison from? Others say they'll put their heads in a gas oven. But there hasn't been any gas for months. My father gave me a razor before he went back to the Eastern Front. He told me I must not fall into the hands of the Russians at any cost. But,' her voice faltered, 'I can't use that thing and slit my own throat—'

'Oh my God,' he exclaimed. 'Have things here in the Homeland come down to that?'

She didn't seem to hear. Instead, she said broken-voiced, 'In the end, we don't even know how to kill ourselves—' She could speak no more.

He pulled her slim girl's body tightly to him, feeling her heart pound against his chest, knowing that she was shedding silent tears and knowing too that he could do nothing to help her. She and the rest were alone with their fates. He, for his part, would decide what was going to happen to him on the field of battle. There, he'd have a fifty-fifty chance of beating it.

Down below in the dingy inn corridor, an old clock ticked away the minutes of their lives with metallic inexorability. Time seemed without end, until finally he felt her soft hand with its cunning long fingers slide down the hardness of his stomach to between his open thighs, and heard her voice, still full of tears, whispering, 'Can I excite you ... Perhaps we can make love ... for one last time...'

THE SUPREME COMMANDER

'Even generals sometimes wet their knickers.'
Anon British staff officer, winter 1942

Speedy Valley, Tunisia, Jan 11th 1943

The correspondent of the *Daily Herald* had been right. General Fredendall, the commander of the US Second Corps, was very definitely anti-British. Indeed, it had seemed to 'Crasher' Nichols on that first day that the whole American formation was of the same persuasion. All the staff officers he had encountered that cold afternoon in that strange underground headquarters, so far behind the fighting front in Tunisia, had been decidedly 'Limey-haters'. Perhaps they aped their commander because it would be unwise not to do so, he didn't know. But it had not been a very pleasant feeling to be treated in that manner, especially as the British and Americans were supposed to be fighting on the same side.

The very first US officer he had met after leaving his jeep, a callow young first lieutenant, wearing a woollen jacket, who looked as if he hadn't shaved for a week, though he did carry a brand-new '45 pistol in a fancy shoulder holster, had looked at Nichols as if *he were the proverbial man from Mars.*

'A Britisher,' he'd exclaimed after Nichols had shown his military ID card, orders and the like. 'What's a Britisher doing here? Why, don't you know. This is American territory?'

Nichols might have enlightened him on that score. This was very definitely *not* 'American territory'. If anything, it belonged neither to the Americans nor the French, but to the Arabs, who had been there first. But he desisted, thinking it was wiser to avoid argument at this stage of his temporary attachment by Montgomery and Eisenhower personally to General Fredendall's green US corps. Instead, he had listened patiently as the flustered young staff officer had phoned up the staff chain to report his presence at the HQ, as if it demanded a major high-level decision. Once, he had seen him put his hand over the mouthpiece of the field telephone and add to his report, 'Looks like some kind of Limey fag to me, Colonel.' He had understood the 'Limey', but the 'fag' had puzzled him. He told himself that he had not realized the Yanks used the English slang word for 'cigarette', though what role it played in this context was beyond him.

That night he had still not seen the commanding general. Instead, he had eaten like some kind of outcast in the senior officers' underground 'chow-hall', isolated from his

American fellow-colonels, who concentrated on their evening meal, three times the size of that served in a British officers' mess, which they wolfed down in silence, even the ice cream, a delicacy that Nichols had not seen these many years. But then, conversation would have been damned difficult anyway. For somewhere in the interior of these underground headquarters, the US engineers were still tunnelling and blasting and making a terrible racket that would go on for most of the night.

Next morning, Nichols was finally admitted to the great man's presence. He gave the general, slumped in front of a glowing pot-bellied stove in his cave-office, dressed in a woollen jacket, a woollen cap pulled down about his ears, and sucking moodily at his corn cob pipe, the best British salute that he could muster, and reported.

Idly, Fredendall touched his pipe to his GI cap in some kind of acknowledgement and growled, 'Why are you here, Colonel? This is the US zone of operations.'

'I know, sir,' Nichols replied, still standing to attention, for the general had made no attempt to stand him at ease. 'I am supposed to help you.'

Fredendall looked at him directly for the first time, as if abruptly aware of his presence. 'Help me? What kind of help can you give me, Colonel?' His eyes flashed. 'Eh?'

Over the years, Nichols had become accustomed to prickly regular army senior officers. Fredendall's words didn't upset him. Nor did he go on the defensive, as some officers would have done when confronted by an irate corps commander. He reasoned that when he was back at Oxford, occupying a chair and enjoying all the trappings of college that dated back to the Middle Ages, senior generals would have already been put out to pasture: obscure yesterday's men, who sent angry letters to the *Times* and the broadsheet's American equivalents that were never published.

So he explained the strange attack on the Indian Brigade at the Mareth Line by a German special unit in the employ of the Nazi Secret Service, which had obviously been employed – unsuccessfully, as it turned out – to find a weak spot in Montgomery's defences. 'Naturally, sir,' he explained slowly, as if talking to a somewhat backward child, 'any German spoiling attack by the enemy might have upset the Eight Army's plans, but only for a while. A German attack couldn't have stopped General Montgomery indefinitely.'

Fredendall took his pipe out of his tobacco-stained lips, as if about to make an important pronouncement. 'I've heard to the contrary, Colonel.'

'To the contrary, sir?'

'Yeah. They say that General Montgomery of yours, the *victor of El Alamein*, or whatever you call the damned place,' he emphasized the words scornfully, 'why, they say he needs a goddam bucketload of tea and a week just to change his mind.'

Nichols ignored the insult. Neatly he fielded the remark with, 'Well, I must admit the General is very thorough, sir. But then, as a veteran of the slaughter of the Western Front in World War One, he doesn't like to waste his soldiers' lives.'

'Soldiers are there to die, if necessary. That's what they get paid for, Colonel.'

Nichols told himself that it didn't look as if Fredendall would die anywhere else but in bed of old age, by the looks of the underground headquarters he was constructing for himself out here, so far behind the front. 'Anyway, sir,' he continued, 'General Montgomery is of the opinion that Rommel's Germans had found his Mareth Line too tough a nut to crack. He reported this to General Eisenhower in Algiers, who sent for me to hear what I thought about the matter. The upshot, sir, was that the Supreme Commander has posted me temporarily to your HQ to help, in any way I can, your own Intelligence staff, who perhaps,' he hesitated momentarily, 'are not quite used to the ways of the Hun as yet.'

Inwardly Nichols smirked. He already knew a lot about Fredendall's intelligence staff. Some of them were smart young recent graduates from Harvard. The rest were middle-aged, pot-bellied 'retreads', as the Yanks called them: civilians who had been in France in the old war and had last used their intelligence talents in 1918, and had been recalled after Pearl Habour. He feared they wouldn't know much about the kind of blitzkrieg warfare the Germans employed in the desert.

Still, Fredendall was now impressed. The name of Supreme Commander Eisenhower had done it. For the Second Corps Commander knew that he was now the second oldest US commander in the field. He'd never get a second chance if he failed in combat now. Everything, his whole future and the promotion to lieutenant-general he craved, depended upon Ike, who had personally asked him to take over Second Corps. Perhaps this Limey officer, who definitely looked like a 'fag', with his handkerchief up the sleeve of his tunic and the way he used his delicate white hands, had been sent by Ike to do him a good turn.

Somewhat mollified, he said, 'Well, Colonel, what exactly are you proposing to do here at my HQ?'

'I'm not going to interfere, sir, in the daily work of your excellent Intelligence staff, I can assure you of that. You could say, sir, that I'm going to hold a watching brief. Keep a lookout for anything in the way of covert ops by the Germans, which might indicate they're about to attack your corps.'

Fredendall pulled a face. Again he pointed the stem of his pipe at Nichols, almost as if he half-intended to spear him with it. 'Colonel, in the Second Corps we don't get attacked, *we attack*!'

And that was that...

Some forty-eight hours later, after surveying the Second Corps positions, 'Crasher' Nichols was no longer so sanguine about it and its commanding general. The soldiers were green, and although they looked soldierly in their brand-new uniforms and helmets, which they wore all the time, unlike Montgomery's men of the Eighth Army, they never seemed to post air lookouts or sentries, often stacking their rifles, whereas experienced combat soldiers would never be without a weapon.

Fredendall's staff were no better. They kept proposing bold plans of attack to please the corps commander, but neglected to reconnoiter the ground to check whether it was suitable for vehicles or armour; it was clear that the American Army didn't 'hike' any-where, as they called it. Instead they always used 'wheels' – but not enough to check the lie of the land. More often when Nichols and his handsome young driver took a look at the terrain themselves, they found it was unsuitable for vehicles or, as the former 'Cherry-picker' put it, 'A couple of Jerries with a machine gun and lad to carry the ammo could hold off a battalion of Yanks up in those hills from here to eternity.'

Yet despite the Americans' lack of experience and concentration on plans which were not implemented, the Germans had not yet made any moves against the Second Corps. All the same, Nichols was receiving top secret messages and signals from both Monty's and the British First Army head-quarters, indicating that the German threat was growing.

For Nichols was privy to the greatest secret of the war. It was that British boffins in Bletchley Park in the Home Counties were tapping the secret German Enigma coding device. The German decodes indicated that the enemy was planning an attack, sending whatever reserves and resources they could spare from the Russian front to North Africa. Already the British chief of the Bomber Command, the hard-nosed 'Bomber' Harris, was attempting to destroy all rail links from the Reich to the Mediterranean. There the Navy was waiting to do what they could to prevent whatever got through from reaching North African ports that were still in German hands; it was clear from the location of the ports to which men and munitions were going that the enemy was about to attack the Americans. But where?

Here at Supreme HQ in Algiers, opinions were divided, though most of the intelligence and staff officers in the know thought the enemy would assault Fredendall's Second Corps. Nichols thought the same. Fredendall, occupied with building his funkhole to the rear, was wide open for an attack. But where? That was the problem. But already Nichols had concluded that wherever the Germans attempted a reconnaissance in force, it would be there that they would attack...

Hotel St Georges, Algiers, Jan 13th 1943

General Eisenhower stubbed out one of the sixty Camels he smoked a day and immediately lit another. Around him in the pale winter sunlight that filtered through the large window of the top-class Algerian hotel which now served as his headquarters, his staff, British and American, waited. They could tell he was in a bad mood. For the customary ear-to-ear smile which was becoming known throughout the Western world was absent this January day.

The Supreme Commander took one last glance at the smooth sea below and turned to face his staff. Outside, a truck-load of GIs was heading north, presumably for the front. They were bellowing a chorus of the current US Army ditty about *'dirty Gertie from Bizert-e'*. No one laughed. Taking the sombre mood from the big American general, they didn't feel it very wise even to smile. When Eisenhower was in this kind of humour, he had a razor-sharp temper; he'd fire a staff officer at the drop of a hat.

'I hear, gentlemen,' the Supreme Commander commenced, 'from the Intelligence people at Fredendall's HQ, that they are expecting the Krauts to attack – if they *do* attack, though I personally don't think they will – through the mountain passes into the plain beyond, held by Second Corps. Now, Fredendall's Intelligence hasn't informed me of this, but my own man there *has.*'

He paused significantly, though no one dared enquire who his 'man' at Fredendall's HQ was. 'General Anderson here,' he indicated the tall, austere commander of his British First Army, 'who has had plenty of experience of the Germans in both wars, if I may say so.'

Anderson's dour expression didn't change. The Scot had no vanity and no charisma either.

'Well, Anderson has warned us often enough how quickly the Nazis react in attack. Within a couple of hours of capturing a position, they'll have it organized for defence. We are not in the same class. So, what conclusion can one draw from that? This,' he answered his own question. 'We must have our defensive positions prepared in advance. Fredendall, who is a very good officer, though he believes solely in attack and defence, has not done that. He has no wire up. No minefield planted and no real anti-tank guns dug in in prepared gunpits.' He paused for breath, while Anderson, who had already suffered a defeat at the hands of von Arnim's Fifth Panzer Army and was now bogged down in the thick mud, waiting for better weather before he could attack again, nodded his head in sombre agreement.

'Not only that,' Eisenhower continued. 'I must inform you, gentlemen, that General Fredendall has got his troops pretty badly mixed up. His First Armored and the Thirty-Fourth Infantry are totally mixed together, which would make it difficult if we needed the armour for any counter-strike against an enemy attack.' He looked at Anderson and added, 'As you British say, he's got his troops spread all over the place in penny packets. It seems that all Second Corps dispositions have been made on the basis of his maps, instead of looking at the terrain.' Eisenhower refrained from telling his listeners that the reason was simple. Fredendall had still to make a personal visit to his troops in the front line; he seemed more concerned with building his underground fortress to the rear. It wouldn't have done, Eisenhower reasoned, to have explained to the staff that Fredendall appeared to be more concerned with his own safety than the battle to come. Indeed, his 'man' had informed him from Second Corps Headquarters, that Fredendall seemed mortally afraid of being bombed. Every time that an aircraft flew over his HQ, according to his source, Fredendall would look up fearfully and exclaim, as if he really meant it, 'I hope that's one of ours!'

Eisenhower let his words sink in. Most of the staff officers there had never been to the front in Tunisia; indeed, only a handful of the American ones present had ever been in combat, and that had been in 1918, or more recently against what they called the second team', the French, who had defended their coast line against the invading Anglo-Americans for three days, inflicting a thousand casualties on their supposed 'liberators'. They thought of the front as some remote place inhabited by a totally different breed of soldiers. Now Eisenhower surprised them by announcing, 'I think it's about time, gentlemen, that you and I had a look at the Second Corps front personally.'

His statement caused quite a sensation among the staff. Even Anderson, who always tried to lead from the front, expressed surprise. Ever since he had teamed up with the Americans the previous November when they had invaded North Africa, he had got quite used to the Yanks of the staff never visiting the front, living instead in palatial headquarters way behind the lines, like the French and English generals had done in the First World War. 'I say, sir, is that wise?' he exclaimed.

Eisenhower forced a laugh, though he had never felt less like laughing. For he knew that if he failed here in Africa, he'd be returned to the States; he wouldn't get a second bite at the cherry. 'It may not be wise, General,' he answered, 'but it's something I've got to do. I know it is not the tradition or custom in our army for a senior officer to comment on dispositions made by a local commander of lower rank. But I just want to be sure that we're ready in the Second Corps area for any German attack that may materialize, though as I have said already, I don't think that attack will materialize. The Krauts are beat and they know it. From now onwards, when we and Monty getting moving again, the enemy will simply pull back – that's my guess.'

Anderson wasn't convinced. He felt that Eisenhower and these new boys from over the Atlantic simply didn't know just how resilient the Huns were. But he didn't air that thought. Instead he said, 'Well, look after yourself, sir.' For a man of his severe nature, that was high emotion indeed, and Eisenhower knew it. He said with a chuckle, 'Don't worry, general, I value my own skin very highly. Now then, gentlemen, this is what I'm going to do...'

Kasserine Pass, Jan 14th 1943

'Cherry-picker – Bandit ... at three o'clock!'
The young ex-Eleventh Hussar at the wheel of Nichols's jeep reacted at once. Veteran that he was, he knew instinctively what to do. Wildly he swung the jeep's steering wheel round to the left, and the little vehicle crashed from the steep rocky mountain track and slammed into the camel thorn to the side, some ten yards away, its engine stalled.

Just in time. Next moment, the little German monoplane came swinging lazily over the rise to their right, as if it had all the time in the world. Nichols breathed hard, as he crouched close to the sergeant. It was a Fies-ler Storch spotter plane, and it was searching for something at just above stalling speed.

'What do you make of it, sir?' his compan-ion asked, keeping his face to the ground. Accustomed to the desert war, he knew the pilot would spot his face set against the over-all yellow-brown of the terrain all around them.

As the spotter plane came roaring in even lower, dragging a whirling prop-wash of sand behind it, Nichols ducked hastily, touc-hing the ground with his face. Voice muffled, he replied, 'It's obvious. The Jerry's doing a recce of that pass up there ... And it's clear that it's not just a routine check. He would not waste so much time—'

He stopped short as the first black egg tumbled from the side of the Storch and exploded in a burst of flame and a furious eruption of sand some twenty or so yards away.

'The bugger's spotted us,' the 'Cherrypick-er' yelled as the Storch flew over them, its prop-wash lashing and whipping their uniforms about their skinny bodies.

'And he's coming in for another bloody go,' Nichols shouted, knowing now that it was no use trying to hide any longer; they had been well and truly spotted. And for some reason, the pilot was determined to wipe them out. He sat up. Next to him, the 'Cherrypicker' did the same. Hastily, he unslung his sub-machine gun. Routinely, he tapped the magazine to check whether it was attached correctly. It was. Now the two of them sat there in the sand, making no attempt to hide, waiting to take up the challenge as the Storch came closer and closer, racing across the floor of the desert.

This time, the lone pilot had a surprise for them. Just as he reached the area of yellow, parched scrub grass, he did something totally unexpected. He dropped a jerrican of petrol. It slammed into the ground. Immediately the petrol started to leak out of it and flood the grass, as the air was suddenly full of its stink.

'What the hell—' the 'Cherrypicker' cried. Then he got it. 'The bastard's gonna try to burn us out, sir. Look.'

In that very same moment, the German flung a grenade, directly into the middle of the petrol-soaked grass. It ignited at once. At first it was merely a series of tiny blue flames, but in the stiff wind that always seemed to blow through the Kasserine Pass, the flames started to rise. They began to advance on the two men crouched there, and even as the heat started to strike them in the faces, Nichols knew there was no use trying to make a run for it. The pilot would gun them down before they'd gone a dozen yards. They had to knock the bastard out of the sky – or else.

Next to him the 'Cherrypicker' rose to his feet. To Nichols at that moment, he seemed like a latter-day David facing up to an aerial Goliath – and a very handsome David too. He said a quick prayer that the young soldier would pull it off.

Now the Storch seemed to fill the sky in front of them. Nichols could see the pilot enshrined in his plastic canopy, quite clearly – a hard-faced, jaw-set German wearing over-large flying goggles. Nichols knew what the German expected. As the flames came ever closer – he thought they'd run for it, and then they would be sitting ducks. But the pilot hadn't reckoned with the 'Cherrypicker'. The young man tensed. Nichols could see his fingers whiten as he took the pressure on the Sten gun's trigger. It was now or never. The plane was almost upon them.

Suddenly, startlingly so that Nichols jumped, the 'Cherrypicker' fired. And he didn't miss. Abruptly the cockpit canopy shattered into a gleaming spider's web. The pilot clutched at his chest. In the very last instant, he caught the plane as it started to fall, dark smoke pouring from its damaged engine. The 'Cherrypicker' showed no mercy. 'Drop, you swine!' he called, and fired again.

'Take that!'

Blinded behind his shattered cockpit, blood pouring from his chest, the pilot tried and failed to keep control. Suddenly he slumped forward over the joystick, perhaps dead or unconscious. The damaged plane slipped to the left, smoke pouring from it now.

The two Englishmen realized that the grass fire was almost upon them. If the plane crashed into it, there'd be one hell of a conflagration. 'Come on,' Nichols yelled urgently, suddenly aware of the danger. 'Let's bloody well run for it!'

The 'Cherrypicker' needed no urging. They ran back in the direction of the stalled jeep. The 'Cherrypicker' flung himself behind the wheel. The Storch was forgotten. He started the engine. It sprang on immediately. 'Back out!' Nichols cried, as to their right, the Storch smashed down with an impact that made the ground all about tremble.

'Fucking thing,' the 'Cherrypicker' cursed, the sweat pouring down his face. Next to him, Nichols willed the jeep to get out of the rut which was preventing them from moving on. Then, as the crackling blue flames were almost upon them, the jeep moved. In a great spurt of sand, its wheels giving off the stench of burned rubber, they moved. The

'Cherrypicker' didn't waste time. He slammed home first gear, and then they were heading forward, hell-for-leather for the crashed, smoking Storch.

The driver hit the brakes automatically. 'Oh, my God!' he gasped.

Next to him, Nichols would have liked to have expressed his horror, too. But he was a senior officer and he restrained himself. Something was staggering towards them. Nichols forced himself to look at the pilot who had somehow fought his way out of the wrecked plane, as he advanced upon them.

Instead of a face, the 'thing' (and now Nichols could think of the dying pilot only as a 'thing' and not a human being) possessed a black crushed mask, through which the naked flesh below showed in blood-red cracks. Where the eyes should have been, there were two vivid purple pools. With agonizing slowness, one charred hand outstretched, through which the bones gleamed like polished ivory, it tottered blindly towards them.

Slowly, very slowly, Nichols's right hand fell to his pistol holster.

Still it came on, its brilliant red hole of a mouth uttering strange animal-like sounds. Once it stumbled. Somehow it righted itself and came on in that obscene stiff manner, the charred hand extended, as if it meant to touch the faces of the two petrified Englishmen.

Then it stopped, as if it sensed, blinded though it was, that they were within reaching distance. Brave as they were, hardened to the horror of war, they flinched and pulled back. Suddenly Nichols felt sick at the thought that it might reach out with that charred limb, which looked like a black-burnt, gnarled branch. It opened the hole that had once served it as a mouth. Meaningless sounds emerged from it as it swayed there wildly, its flesh hanging in dull-red stripes, swaying back and forth. 'Don't...' It uttered the word in English. '*Bitte*—' It didn't complete the plea, but Nichols understood the broken-off German. It wanted him to shoot it.

He hesitated, the hot bile flooding his throat. He knew he was going to vomit uncontrollably in a moment if he didn't do something. Almost without knowing, he levelled his pistol and clicked off the safety catch.

'*Bitte*—' The plea changed to a howl of absolute pain, as Nichols fired and the bullet struck it squarely in the chest. At that range, the impact was tremendous. The German was swept completely off his feet, stick-like arms flailing in a sudden mad fury. Nichols gasped. Now, for the first time, he saw the black and white armband on the mutilated monster's right sleeve. It read *'REGIMENT BRANDENBURG'*.

Next moment he couldn't contain himself any longer. His skinny body heaved. Then he was doubled up, retching violently, as if he would never stop...

Eisenhower's mobile HQ in the field, south west Tunisia, Jan 20th 1943

The general's staff worked all-out to hide the general's bottles. They liked the 'Old Man', as they called the veteran of the Great War, but they knew that an old lush, as he had become over the boring years since 1918, should have never been sent overseas on active service. He just wasn't up to commanding troops in the field, especially such green draftees and the like, that he now led – 'drugstore cowboys and canteen commandos', as the West Pointers on the staff called them contemptuously.

Still, the old general was their commander and they felt a sense of loyalty. Besides, they knew if the Supreme Commander knew the true state of the general, not only would his head roll, but some of theirs too. As the chief-of-staff had told them grimly when they had discovered the CG sprawled out on his cot with a half-empty bottle of bourbon clutched in his hand, 'Don't be fooled by

Ike, gentlemen. Behind that smile of his, there is a tough guy who won't stop at nothing. If he finds out what's been going on here, the chief'll go, and some of us, particularly me, for not having reported what a mess the CG is.'

Now, while the staff searched the Commanding General's quarters for bottles, empty or otherwise, the divisional surgeon worked to try to sober him up before Eisenhower and his entourage arrived. He had already tried plenty of hot coffee and attempting to make his patient sick. Both of the traditional methods had failed. In truth, the General had regained a sort of consciousness, but he seemed to believe that he was still in the trenches in France back in 1918, rapping out nonsensical orders about 'going over the top' and 'giving the heinies hell, boys, for the sake of the good ole regiment'. A couple of times he had burst into that ribald ditty of the time about the elderly French lady who *'has never been fucked for twenty years … inky-pinky parlez vous'*.

Now the sweating, angry divisional surgeon was slapping the CG about the face to bring him round, and considering whether to give him such a big shot of dope that it would either sober him up or kill him. At that moment, he was so furious with his high-ranking patient that he couldn't care what the damned result was.

A few miles away Eisenhower's car, driven by his green-eyed Irish chauffeuse Kay Summersby, had halted, with his guard of MPs, armed with tommy guns, spread out rapidly to form a defensive perimeter, though according to Intelligence there was not a German within a radius of twenty miles. Approaching from the south-west, another small convoy of high-ranking staff officers was approaching. In the lead came Corps Commander Fredendall and his senior staff. For some reason, since Eisenhower had last welcomed Fredendall to his new post as Second Corps Commander, he and his staff had shaved their heads to show that they were real combat soldiers. For his part, Eisenhower thought, as he whispered to Kay, who was more than a mere driver, 'they look like a lot of goddam movie Indians, for Chrissake, Kay'.

She giggled. A few moments later he and Fredendall, who had taken off his stocking cap to reveal the full beauty of his grey, shaven head, were shaking hands.

For a moment or two they 'shot the breeze', as Fredendall expressed it, before Eisenhower got down to business with a brisk, 'Well, General, what do you think of your defensive position up here?' He indicated the two prominent hills to their front which defended the pass. 'Those Djebels up there, for instance. Eh?'

Fredendall, who had never been this far up the front as yet, and knew the position only from his study of the maps of the area, was as foolishly confident as ever. 'All well in hand, General,' he replied. 'I've placed two formations from Ward's First Armored Division on each hilltop. Ideal defensive position. As we were taught at the Point, whatever happens, if the Krauts do attempt to break through and even succeed, we can hold the shoulders and attack them from the flank.'

Eisenhower wasn't particularly impressed; still he didn't like to tell a senior corps commander how to do his job. 'But are they mutually supporting? I've been told they're ten miles apart.'

'Don't you worry your head about that, General,' Fredendall assured him. 'Old Al's in charge of the two features and you know him? He might be slow, but he's a goddam dogged fighter.' He turned and shouted the name that the staff of the alcoholic general were dreading, 'Send up Old Al, toot sweet, will you?'

A moment or two of fussing as the staff handed the general a peppermint to suck and splashed some aftershave lotion on his florid face to remove the last traces of alcohol, and then the CG was advancing towards

Eisenhower, slow but ramrod-straight like the old soldier that he was.

He paused the regulation six paces in front of the Supreme Commander. Behind him, his worried staff tensed. Slowly he raised his hand to his cap in salute. Gravely, Eisenhower returned the military greeting. The staff prepared to breathe out with relief while the divisional surgeon murmured under his breath 'Goddamit, I was just about to take up serious drinking myself—' The words died on his lips.

Suddenly the CG had become aware of Eisenhower's pretty red-headed driver. Instantly he forgot Eisenhower. He turned to Miss Summersby and bowed gallantly. For some reason known only to his addled brain, he said in French, perhaps transported to that older war when he had been a virile young officer, *'Bonjour, Ma'mselle, je suis enchante de faire votre connaissance.'* Then, before anyone could stop him, the alcoholic general bent low and gallantly kissed a totally surprised Summersby's hand.

Eisenhower glared at Fredendall, eyes red with rage. 'Goddamit, Fredendall,' he exploded as they stood apart from the others, including the general, who kept saying to his staff in bewilderment, 'But what did I do wrong, gentlemen ... What did I do wrong...?'. 'What kinda goddam outfit are you running up here? Two outfits set on hilltops ten miles apart. If the Krauts attack fast, they could sweep between them and leave your guys up there nice and tidy, ready for the Krauts to collect without trouble and be sent to the POW cages ... Then that lush over there,' he shook his head, as if he couldn't understand the world any more. 'Jesus Christ, how could you let him be in charge of two such important strategic features as those Djebels? If they go, your damned front goes too.'

An unhappy Fredendall appeared to writhe, but not much. As always, he was sure he was right. 'I take your point, sir. Perhaps I have been a bit slack on that score. But I'm not in the business of defence, sir, as you know. I'm just a good ole country boy who flunked out of West Point twice. But if I don't know much about higher strategy, I do know that we Americans don't defend, *we attack*.' He smiled suddenly at a red-faced angry Eisenhower, as if that explained everything. 'Yessir. Attack. The old lush is good enough to hold a defensive position until I'm ready to go on the offensive, I expect you'll agree, sir.'

Eisenhower seemed to be about to blow up. 'No, I don't damn well agree, General. From what I know from my own private intelligence sources, the Germans are actively preparing to attack you. There is no time to waste on drunks like that over there. You want your best men at the front. You want to have your defences in order. You want to be prepared, *not* to attack, but to damn well fend off an attack.' His chest heaved with the effort of talking so much and trying, the best he could, to keep his temper. 'Now for Pete's sake, get on the stick!' With that said, Eisenhower turned and stalked back to the waiting car, not even returning the rigid salutes of the various staffs. As his armoured Packard drew away without Eisenhower looking back he was so angry, the alcoholic general was saying over and over again, 'But what did I do wrong, guys? Just tell me that, what did I do wrong ... ?'

Headquarters, Fifth German Panzer Army, Tunis, Jan 20th 1943

Rommel was writing to his beloved wife Lu in Germany once again. He was back in Africa. But he felt no sense of joy at being reunited with his famed *Afrikakorps*. That formation was a shadow of its former self, deprived of supplies, of men and munitions. Indeed, there were more Italians, whom he despised, fighting among its ranks than Germans.

Once he had been world famous. Hadn't

Churchill himself exclaimed, half in despair, half in admiration, 'Rommel, Rommel, what else matters but beating him?' Well, he knew that he was almost beaten now. But he couldn't just stand there, as sick and as heartbroken as he was, and let his reputation disappear altogether. He owed it to himself, to Germany and, above all, to his loyal survivors of the old, ever-victorious *Afrikakorps*, not to let that happen.

As he wrote now to Lucie Maria in far-off Swabia, 'It's two years today since I arrived on African soil. Two years of heavy and stubborn fighting, most of the time with a far superior enemy. I have endeavoured to do my duty, both in my own sphere and the cause as a whole ... must do our best to beat off the mortal dangers that beset us ... Unfortunately it's all a matter of supplies. I hope my decision to remain with my troops to the end will be confirmed. You will understand my attitude. As a soldier one cannot do otherwise.' He flung the cheap wooden pen down, as if it were suddenly red-hot. There, he had told her. Come what may, even if he had to die in the attempt, he would win one last victory, however short-lived. Without it he did not want to return home. He'd rather make her a widow and his son fatherless and let his bones whiten in the hot sun of Africa.

He looked at his old watch. It was nearly midday. The staff of the Fifth Army would be soon going to their lunch in the officers' mess. He had planned it that way. It would mean he could see *Oberleutnant* Scharf in charge of the Brandenburgers without too many at the big headquarters being aware of the meeting. There were too many loose tongues at von Arnim's headquarters, and even the commanding general of the Fifth Panzer Army was known to be a bit of a chatterbox, who couldn't keep a secret over-long.

With a slight groan of pain, he raised himself from his wood-and-canvas field chair and bellowed, 'Orderly, send in *Oberleutnant* Scharf!'

'Sir.' The orderly, one of his *Afrikankorps* veterans (he wasn't going to have any of von Arnim's troops serving him), smiled and bellowed in return, *'Oberleutnant Scharf, der Generalfeldmarschall lässt bitten!'*

Scharf marched in smartly and clicked to attention, looking like a pre-war regular rather than the member of the *Abwehr's* covert special operations regiment and a civilian pre-war tea planter in far-off British Ceylon. Duly he reported at the top of his voice in the old-style Prussian fashion.

Rommel forced a weary grin. 'I don't know, Scharf, I think you're making a real soldier after all.'

Scharf took in Rommel's yellow face, the desert sores vanished now after treatment in Reich, but still very sickly looking, and grinned himself. 'I think when the time comes, I'd rather turn back to Ceylon and my tea, sir – if I last that long.'

'Of course you will. You know the old German saying, "weeds never die".' His grin vanished. 'All right, Scharf, sit down. There are cigarettes – looted *Ami* ones – and schnapps there if you feel the need. *Obstle**★* from my native Swabia, in fact. Made by my own dear wife herself.'

'Thank you, sir,' Scharf said, but didn't attempt to reach out for the proferred items. By this time, he knew his generals. As young officers they had drunk like fish themselves, but they frowned on young officers doing the same now they were generals. There were others too, who paid life service to the Führer's intense dislike of strong drink and tobacco. He waited.

He didn't have long to do so. Rommel launched straight into his plan. 'Well, you know I can't tackle the British any more. Still, Montgomery has not yet moved – a careful man that, a very careful man. So for

★A schnapps made from various fruits, mainly pear and apple.

a while I fear no threat from the direction of the Mareth Line. But you know all that, Scharf. In the meantime I intend, together with Colonel-General von Arnim's Fifth Panzer, to give this Eisenhower chap and his *Amis* a little shock.'

'You'll attack the Americans, sir?'

'Yes, Scharf.'

Scharf nodded soberly. It was what he had expected. Outside, a platoon of panzer grenadiers were marching past, singing lustily that, *'We were in the east, we were in the west, but the Homeland is the best'*. Rommel frowned momentarily. Perhaps the reference to battles fought in east and west to no avail, and that a soldier would be better off at home, made him conscious of his own position.

Now he continued with, 'I have the feeling, however, that the *Amis* are beginning to suspect that I might attack their positions. After all, our spies tell us that their Supreme Commander, this fellow with the German name—'

'Eisenhower, sir.'

'Yes, Eisenhower has been touring his front in the last few days. A usual sign that a commander is worried or preparing for an imminent attack.'

'I agree they might be concerned about our intentions, sir, if you don't mind my saying so, Field Marshal,' Scharf interrupted. 'We have given them some little reason to do so ourselves.' Swiftly he related the details of the abortive flight over the Faid Pass by one of the Brandenburg pilots, who had been shot down. 'Unfortunately, sir, although the poor chap died after the crash and I don't think the enemy had time to get anything out of him, his sleeve armband and cameras and such like would have revealed that he belonged to Regiment Brandenburg, and they know our role in the desert war.'

'Yes, I know,' Rommel answered, though this was the first time he had, in reality, heard of the plane's crash. 'It is for that very reason that I have called you here to brief you on your next reconnaissance probing mission personally.'

'Sir?'

'I don't want to scare the *Amis* into improving their dispositions at a place called Kasserine, which will be the focal point of our attack, once we have achieved our breakthough. Those passes are damnably difficult to assault as it is. To attack them successfully, we'd need to outnumber the defenders by at least three to one. We cannot achieve that ratio and there's no use discussing crushing the defenders by sheer weight of numbers. Hence we must be devious. Hit them by a route that will come to them by surprise—'

Again he paused as his briefing was disturbed by the rumble and rusty squeak of tanks. Instinctively both of them looked out of the window.

Scharf whistled, awed at what he saw out there. Rommel looked suddenly pleased. Swinging stiffly round the corner came an armoured monster, its great overhanging 88mm cannon nearly knocking holes in the sides of the nearest houses, its massive engines rearing and reverberating down the dusty stone chasm of buildings.

'My secret,' Rommel said proudly. 'You know it?' He raised his voice as the first gigantic tank was followed by another, and yet another.

'Yessir,' Scharf yelled back, very impressed. 'Well, I've heard of them, but didn't know they were here in this theatre of war. The Tiger?'

'Yes, the Tiger. The most powerful tank in the world, all sixty tons of it. No other tank or anti-tank gun that we know about can stop the beast. It is a war-winning weapon. It is a pity we have so few of them for the coming attack on the *Amis*, for when they see the Tiger with their puny anti-tank shells bouncing off its tough steel hide like damned ping-pong balls, they'll tuck their legs under their armpits and run for it. Of that I'm sure.'

Scharf smiled, amused at the Field Marshal's strange image, pleased too that his old hero seemed happy, even temporarily.

'Now,' Rommel forgot the Tigers, 'this is what I want you to do. We must not draw any attention to you. We'll let von Arnim posture if he wants. In the end,' he smiled a little maliciously, 'he'll be my successor out here and end up a prisoner of war, probably behind Tommy barbed wire. So let him have his moment or two of glory. You, I, must proceed as secretly as possible, assuming that it will be the Fifth Panzer Army that will do the attacking in Tunisia and not my *Afrikakorps*. So find my men the best possible route of attack. Go through the back door, one might phrase it, and not through the front one, and catch the *Amis* with their pants down about their fat American ankles. Can you do that for me, Scharf?'

There was a note of almost pleading in the field marshal's voice, and Scharf, not a particularly emotional man, felt his heart go out to him. 'Of course, sir, you can rely on my Brandenburgers.'

The field marshal stretched out his hand. His grip was weak and damp. 'Then *Hals und Beinbruch*,* *Oberleutnant* Major, I wish

*Literally 'break your neck and bones,' ie 'happy landings'.

you all the best.' And that was that. Moments later Scharf found himself outside facing an angry, excited Lieutenant Brandt, whose first words indicated that he couldn't, as he had just informed the field marshal, totally rely on the Brandenburgers. They were, 'That damned swine, *Oberleutnant*, has just deserted.'

'What damned swine?' Scharf asked somewhat absently, his mind full of the field marshal's orders.

'The German-American, sir. Jenkins, sir, he's gone and done a bunk...'

Rue Des Pins, Tunis, Jan 20th 1943

The whore had breathed, 'You want jig-jig, German boy?' She had thrust out her plump stomach provocatively, licking her pink tongue about wet lips. 'Anything you want, German boy ... Round the world, anything?' Her German was good, and he guessed she had been servicing sex-starved German *landsers* for a while in the capital.

Jenkins was half-drunk and broke, yet the antics of the teenage whore excited him. '*Ja*,' he said thickly. 'German boy like jig-jig.'

For a moment she forgot her attempt to entice him. Instead she was businesslike. It was getting dark and she wanted to get as much money as possible out of this German

141

ape, and be off the streets before the German 'chain-dogs' sent her off with a clout of their rubber clubs. 'You pay for jig-jig now?'

'*Jawohl*,' he growled, a little angry that the woman wouldn't drop them and let him get on with the business of the 'beast with two backs', as the soldiers called it. He was without a pass. If the military police, 'the chain dogs'* as they were called, got hold of him without a pass, he'd spend the night in the 'cooler' on bread and frigging water.

'Money,' she demanded, holding out her hand. '*Now!*'

'*Sau!*' he cursed.

She understood the German word, obviously, for she said in the cheeky, determined fashion of a professional whore, '*Nix sau ... Geld.*'

Something snapped in Jenkins. All his life he had never liked being told what to do. Orders angered him, especially as he had been forced to accept so many of them since he had come to Germany and joined the Brandenburgers. In particular, he didn't like pieces of gash telling him what to do, whores at that, who sold their bodies for money, unlike decent women. 'What did you say?' he

---

* *Known thus on account of their silver gorget, attached to a chain that they wore around their necks as a symbol of their office.*

said threateningly, doubling a right fist like a small steam-hammer.

'You hear,' she said, standing her ground. 'Money first, jig-jig after—'

She never finished her demand. He lashed out, brutally. His massive fist smashed into her face, sending her reeling back against the nearest palm tree. She yelped and slumped against it for a moment, trying not to fall, her legs spread as she steadied herself.

'*Salaud*,' she cursed in French, and then in Italian, '*Proce de Madonna*.' She spat out a loose tooth, blood dribbling down the side of her mouth, which was swelling rapidly already. She fought back her tears, knowing that would be fatal. Her clients, many of them bastards like this big hulking German, were swine. They'd do anything if they thought they were in control. Hadn't she been raped by them more times than she cared to count? '*Sal con*,' she swore, 'you pay for this. I call chain-dogs—'

This time a blazing-eyed Jenkins didn't hit her. He shoved her to the ground instead. He felt his loins thicken immediately.

He didn't hesitate. He ripped open his flies. His erection sprang out, red, swollen and ugly. '*Hure*,' he breathed, licking his suddenly dry lips at the sight of her hairy vulva, 'I'll teach you not to talk to me like that.'

'*No*,' she screamed. Her hands flew to her distorted face in horror. 'Please – *NO!*'

He dropped on her, panting like a bull in heat. His weight knocked the breath out of her. She felt she'd black out at any moment. She fought to remain conscious. God knows what this madman might do to her if she passed out. His hands fumbled with her loins. She felt his rough, untrimmed nails thrust themselves inside her. 'Let me,' she said weakly. 'Let me ... you hurt me.'

He wasn't listening. Now he was blind to everything but sexual pleasure and relief. He found what he sought. With a great grunt he thrust himself inside her. She yelled. He didn't notice. He pushed himself even deeper inside her. She writhed back and forth, her frantic hips trying to dislodge him. He didn't hesitate, He slapped her across the face, hard. 'Keep still, bitch, willya?'

Now she was too weak and miserable to fight back any more. He grunted again. Through gritted teeth, he hissed, 'You're going to like this, whore. Now you've got a real man inside you ... So you'd better shut your trap and enjoy it.' Next moment he was thrusting himself in and out of her bruised, bloody body, alone in the world with his own crazy desire and pleasure.

Five minutes later he lay prostrate on her unconscious body, all passion spent, his own

144

limbs lathered in a hot sweat, wishing he could have a stiff drink and then fall asleep. But he knew that couldn't be. He had to be off before the chain-dogs came, or anyone else for that matter. But to where? He'd had a noseful of the shitting Brandenburgers. Risking his neck for pay that wouldn't allow him to hire a cheap foreign whore for a few minutes? What kind of life was that for a red-blooded man?

Anyway, he could see already that the Fatherland had had it here in Africa. They were fighting a last-ditch battle against the Americans, and in the end, his former countrymen would win. They always would with the money these Yid backers possessed to finance their industry. Hell, most Germans were still using horses and carts just as they had done after the First World War, which the Kaiser had lost, and his dad had taken them to the States to lead a better life than they could ever do in a beaten Germany, where the old man worked a solid ten-hour day to buy a loaf of bread, and they pushed his weekly pay of billions of useless marks home in a goddam wheelbarrow.

Suddenly he had it, as he raised himself from her body and stuffed his limp penis back into his pants. He'd go over the hill. Back to the Americans. Americans were kind of simple folks, not as smart as the Europeans. They'd believe anything if you told it right. But he'd need money. Even as the thought flashed through his evil mind, Jenkins knew where he'd get that money. From the unconscious whore.

Hastily he bent over her, wondering where she kept the earnings of this night's work 'pounding the pavement', as the Germans said. He guessed she'd be like all the whores he'd ever known – cunning ... devious. She wouldn't keep it in the cheap sling bag she had suspended from her shoulder as a symbol of her trade, just like some of them wandered around 'on business' with silly little hounds.

But where else?

Swiftly he ran his fingers around her inert frame. She would not have the money tucked in her drawers, because she hadn't worn any. Her bra. Nothing! Somewhere in the distance, he could hear the steady determined tread of heavy boots. Instinctively he knew what that indicated: a patrol of the chain-dogs. 'Great crap on the Christmas tree,' he cursed angrily and redoubled his search. Then he had it. Tucked neatly under her long flowing hair, near the nape of her neck there was a tight wad of notes, secured by some sort of tape.

He acted. Time was running out – fast. He tugged hard. The notes came free. She uttered a small cry of pain and stirred. 'Hold your water, you sow,' he hissed, then as an afterthought, remembering that both the local currency and the German Occupation mark were basically worthless, he jerked hard at the bracelets that adorned her thin wrists. They'd be worth something.

'What—' she began, sitting up. She didn't get far. Stuffing the loot inside his pockets with both hands, he aimed a tremendous kick at her chin with his cruelly shed, heavy 'dice-beaker'.* Something clicked like a bone breaking, and she reeled back to hit the pavement with a sickening thud.

Jenkins didn't even notice. He was too concerned to get away before the chain-dogs arrived. A moment later he was running all out. Behind he left the young prostitute, already beginning to stiffen in a death rigor as the night cold closed in. Now he was no longer just a hunted deserter, but a murderer, too...

* *German Army slang for the jackboot.*

INTO THE DEVIL'S GARDEN

'The ground is miserable. Its water is blood. Its air is poison. You may live there a hundred years without making a friend.'

Old Arab Song

The Devil's Garden, Tunisia, 21st Jan 1943

By midnight on the day that they heard of the murder committed by the deserter Jenkins, they were ready. Scharf knew they could have used the mechanics stationed at von Arnim's Fifth Panzer Army HQ for the task, but he had preferred that his own men should prepare the enemy vehicles for the hard journey to come on the morrow. The fewer people who knew what his Brandenburgers were about, the better.

So behind the locked doors of the hangar-like motor transport sheds, they had laboured hard to prepare one captured US Staghound armoured car, six booty jeeps and a Dodge truck taken from Montgomery's Eighth Army the year before, as transport into what Fifth Army Intelligence called the 'Devil's Garden.'

'At least, that's what the local Arabs call it,' the smart young captain had informed him when Scharf had appealed to him for what information he could supply. 'It's not really desert, so they say. Indeed, in winter when it rains near the coast, it can turn into a sea of mud, as we have found out. But it's feature-less like the desert, and when it doesn't rain it's as barren and waterless as the Sahara is. Naturally there's nothing in the way of settlements with supplies of food and fuel out there. If you're stuck for either, you're in trouble once you've left the litteral area. It's dead man's country really. That's why neither we nor the enemy has used it.' He gave a little shudder. 'I once spent a couple of days out there on a recce for the commanding general and I soon realized why the Arabs call it the Devil's Garden. It's the real arsehole of the world.' He had flashed Scharf a look. 'God knows why anyone in his right mind ever wants to go into it.'

But Scharf, as cautious as ever, didn't enlighten him on that score.

'Well, Brandt,' Scharf said as they finished at midnight and he treated the weary men in their oil-stained overalls to beer and *bockwurst* bought with his own money, the only luxury they'd see, he knew, for many a day to come. 'How does it look?'

The one-armed lieutenant, whose fate had already been sealed, was his normal enthusiastic self, happy to be in combat once more. 'Excellent, sir, I think the vehicles are pretty certain to be runners come what may, and I think, too, we can take care of most eventualities.'

Scharf laughed and said, 'Glauber's Salts?'

The young officer looked puzzled, 'Glauber's Salts, sir?' he echoed.

'Yes, if you run out of good water and have to use the local stuff you find in wells and the like. Glauber's Salts will purify most water.' He clapped the other man over his skinny shoulders. 'Don't worry, I'm sure you have taken care of everything perfectly.'

'I hope so, sir.'

Two hours later, the little convoy of former enemy vehicles set off under a full silver moon, the streets of the capital deserted save for patrols of the chain-dogs, with here and there a group of panzer grenadiers guarding a stationary tank, warming their hands on a fire of logs. No one took any notice of them, even though they were driving enemy vehicles, and they were not challenged a single time. To Scharf it seemed as if they were some kind of ghosts, which remained unseen to the eyes of those who were staying behind. Young Brandt was more direct. 'They don't appear to notice us, sir,' he said, slightly puzzled. 'I wonder why.'

'We're Brandenburgers, Lieutenant. We spell trouble. Nobody in his right mind wants to be associated with doom merchants like us.'

Brandt shuddered.

A little later they paused on the edge of

Tunis while the convoy closed up and a last check was made on the vehicles and their equipment. For after this, they would steer clear of both German military and civilians. If anything went wrong, they would have to rectify the fault themselves, or else ... It was a thought that the Brandenburgers didn't like to follow to its logical conclusion.

It was not far off dawn now. The stars were disappearing, and there was that un-African pre-dawn chill in the air which made Scharf shiver as he smoked his last cigarette in Tunis. Ahead, the open countryside, camel thorn, scrub and rocks still lay covered in darkness. The area might be empty of human beings for kilometres to the south-west; it might be packed with them, waiting for the little band of special troops to make their appearance. Scharf didn't know. He told himself he was being fanciful, letting his nerves get on top of him. He had been on worse and more dangerous reconnaissance missions than this. All the same, he shivered a little as Brandt appeared suddenly out of the shadows to report, 'everything in order, sir. Men and vehicles, though the *Ami* armoured car's leaking oil a bit.' He added, 'Sorry I startled you, sir.'

Scharf forced a smile. 'No, it wasn't you. Spect a louse ran over my grave, that's all. Made me shudder.'

154

'Spect so, sir,' Brandt agreed, though to him, Scharf didn't look one bit as if he were jumpy and given to nerves.

Scharf tossed away his cigarette end in a glowing arc that died almost immediately once it hit the cold sand below. 'All right, Lieutenant. We'd better roll.'

'Yessir,' the young officer agreed enthusiastically. He appeared to be in a hurry to be on his way into the unknown, but then, the Brandenburger commander told himself, all this was an adventure for Brandt. Young men always thought war was an adventure until it became serious and Death began to wave its scythe. *'Los,'* he cried. *'Aufsetzen.'* He waited a moment until the last of those taking a leak at the sides of their vehicles did so and mounted them. Then he gave the final order. *'Gruppe – MARSCH!'*

Everywhere the motors coughed into throaty life, like chesty old men waking up to their first coughing fit of the day. The air was suddenly full of the stink of petrol. Wheels squeaked. Gears protested. And they were moving forward, leaving the familiar security of the capital behind them, heading for the vast waste ahead and the unknown to come.

That first day was easy. The road was good. It had been built by the colonial power before the war, and had been well maintained until the fighting in North Africa had

155

started. Then, it seemed, the white *colons* who had farmed the immediate area had fled back to the capital, leaving their white-painted farms to run to seed or be occupied by the locals, some of whom had pitched their tents in the middle of modern farmyards, living like their forefathers had done for centuries, surrounded by buildings with all modern conveniences.

Scharf was not concerned with the former possessions of the *colons*. His worry was the road, which had been neglected, with unfilled bomb craters here and there, which would have snapped the axles of his vehicles in an instant if one of his drivers were careless enough to drive into one.

About mid-afternoon, the tarmac road gave out, to be replaced by track. But the ground was firm, and as there had not been any rain for a week or so along the coast, there was no mud to worry them. So, apart from soft patches here and there, they were able to maintain a fair speed, and a pleased Scharf was happy to note that he wasn't using up as much precious fuel as he had anticipated. That night as they set up their camp, he allowed Brandt to announce there'd be a ration of good Munich beer to celebrate. There'd be a bottle of Lowenbrau for every two men, and a Bavarian weisswurst apiece to go with it. The weary men cheered, and later slept like logs. Again Scharf was pleased. The men would need to stay in a good mood, for on the morrow they would start into the hills on what was marked on his map as 'easy ascent': something that he couldn't believe possible. For already his maps were proving unreliable. Seemingly, they were more the product of a fertile imagination than that of a real trained mapmaker.

About two that morning, Scharf, as tired as he was, awoke. For a while he lay there gazing at the silver stars, which seemed endlessly remote, mulling over what he intended for the morrow. He heard a soft cough. It was Brandt doing his share of sentry duty like any private soldier. 'All right?' Scharf asked.

Brandt, huddled in a greatcoat, soldier's rifle slung over his shoulder (though how he would use it with only one arm, Scharf didn't know) said, 'Can't you sleep, sir?' He seemed genuinely concerned, and Scharf told himself what a decent young officer he was.

'Oh, yes, I'm all right,' he answered. 'I was just thinking things over, Brandt, planning tomorrow, you know.'

'I see, sir. I was thinking too as I did my spell. These lonely night sentry duties give you time to think, in fact they seem to encourage you to do so.'

'And what were you thinking?'

'Jenkins, sir.'

'Jenkins, Brandt. How do you mean?'

'Well, sir, we know he's done a bunk and that he'll be charged with murdering that poor girl if he ever falls into German hands again. So what's he going to do?'

The question was posed quietly and without emotion. But it struck Scharf as if someone had just punched him in the guts. 'Holy strawsack, Brandt, I see what you mean. The swine.' Almost instantly he was wide awake, mind flooding with boundless possibilities, each one worse than the other.

'I mean, sir,' Brandt put his thoughts into words, 'I wouldn't put it past him to betray us. He's that kind of a swine, out for number one.'

Scharf didn't say anything. Instead he lay back down and pulled the mouth of the sleeping bag higher up about his face. But he was not fated to sleep any more that night.

Next morning they set off once more, again at dawn. Now, however, the country began to change. The hard, dead-straight track gave way to rough broken terrain, dotted with its flat-topped djebels, which looked as if they might have been inhabited once before erosion had worn away the surface earth. Now, however, there was no sign of any human being or human habitation. There was not even the small game that one sometimes caught sight of in the parched grass and scrub.

Their progress, too, was hampered by the rises, and they started to slow down, and Scharf began to worry that they were using too much fuel driving in low gear. But there was not much that he could do about that, save to lighten the load in the vehicles by making the men, protest though they did, walk when they were confronted with yet another uphill climb.

That evening the men were only too eager to eat and sleep. Old hares that most of them were in desert warfare, save for the new German-American recruits (who obviously hadn't expected to be faced with such conditions despite their Brandenburg training back in the Reich), the men soon had their petrol-and-sand fires burning in old cans. Within minutes, thick rich stews made of tins of 'Old Man' and anything else they could find to throw into the mix, especially blocks of dehydrated peas, were bubbling away merrily, giving off that odour of their favourite 'fart soup'.

Wolfing it down with great hunks of *Kommissbrot*, dark bread wrapped in silver paper that was supposed to last for ever, they sat around the dying fires happily like a bunch of great hulking unshaven boy scouts, already beginning to rumble noisily as the peas started to have their effect. Indeed, Sergeant Hartmann was so carried away by the good food and company that he volunteered to give one of his celebrated 'fart concerts', even managing to perform the British *God Save the Queen* with a clever use of wet farts that brought him the applause of all present. Even the German-Americans, who were a straight-laced bunch, very much concerned with personal hygiene and obviously not used to such lavatorial humour, applauded when Hartmann finally concluded with a particularly beautiful high-pitched fart.

Standing at the back, sipping the hot ersatz coffee made of acorns, and smoking his old pipe, Scharf smiled happily. These were the good times out of war, he told himself, which made up for all the hard ones. At times such as these, a man realized he was fighting not out of hatred or for some great cause, but simply for the cameraderie and good fellowship of his 'heap': his fellow soldiers, who often meant more to him than blood relatives. It was for them they died, if they had to die, not for some vague ideology called the 'New Order' or the Führer's vaunted political creed, National Socialism.

For a moment or two, he thought of his hero Erwin Rommel, in this context. Was he fighting for Hitler or to save his own ruined reputation? Or was he, too, on a larger scale, battling on for the same sort of cameraderie – that of his battered old *Afrikakorps*?

Scharf yawned. He knocked the warm dottle out of his old shag-pipe, savoured the aroma for a last few moments and then commanded, 'All right, Lieutenant and you, too, Hartmann, the fart concert's over. Hit the hay and post sentries. We'll need all the shut-eye we can get. Tomorrow's probably going to be tougher than today...'

Wearily they said their goodnights to each other. Here and there, some of those who still had the energy dug holes for their hips with their entrenching tools before slipping into the comforting warmth of their sleeping bags. For already it was beginning to get really cold, Something which had surprised Scharf when he had first arrived in Africa. After the murderous heat of the day, the nights were, startlingly, freezing cold; one might have thought that one was on the Eastern Front in Russia, and not Africa.

Scharf yawned again and told himself he'd be fast asleep within minutes of crawling into his sleeping bag. But that wasn't to be just yet. He felt a familiar rumbling in his gut. He was forced to break wind. *'Verdammte Scheisse,'* he cursed. 'Damned fart soup'. It was the peas; they were going through him swiftly as they always did. He needed to evacuate his bowels. Cursing, he fumbled for some lavatory paper, calling over to Brandt, who was busy arranging the night's sentry roster, 'Going to take a shovel for a walk, Lieutenant.'

'Sir,' Brandt called back dutifully, as Scharf wrenched a shovel from its clip on the side of the captured English Dodge. Paper in one hand, shovel in the other, he plodded through the freezing sand up a little hillock until he was out of sight of the circle of vehicles below. The rumbling in his stomach grew louder. Hurriedly, he dropped the shovel and ripped open his pistol belt. But even in his urgency, he didn't forget to take out the pistol itself and cock it. It was an old fear of his to be caught squatting with his pants around his ankles, being confronted by some grinning Tommy, ordering, 'All right Jerry, get yer hands up. You're a bleeding prisoner of war, mate.'

Next instant he had loosened his belt, dropped his pants, and with a sigh of relief started to carry out the necessary business, hoping that he was not going to suffer a case of the 'thin shits' due to his overindulgence in these damned peas.

But even as he squatted there, groaning a little with both pain and pleasure, he had started surveying what he took to be motor tracks in the vanishing light. As far as he could make out, they started elsewhere and ended here, just above his little camp below. For a moment or two the thought alarmed him. Had some enemy patrol watched their arrival and then thought it wiser to do a bunk and report back to base before they had been spotted?

A second or so later, he told himself he was being a damned fool. The tracks were old. At close range, he could see where sand particles had drifted into the deep marks made by heavy rubber tyres. That indicated the marks had been made long before the Brandenburgers' little convey had arrived.

With a grunt of satisfaction, he noted he wasn't suffering from the 'thin shits' after all. Swiftly he carried out the usual routine, finishing by concealing his faeces with the shovel. He had completed the business of 'taking a shovel for a walk'. All the same, he didn't hurry back to the camp and his waiting sleeping bag. Instead, he thrust the shovel over his shoulder like a rifle and climbed up the hillock a little further, following the tracks.

They didn't go far, but ended fifty or sixty or so metres away, where a patch of glistening dark brown indicated where oil had leaked from one of the unknown vehicles' sump. He bent and touched it. It was almost dry. It had been there a fair while. He stared at the tyre tracks themselves. They were definitely enemy. Only the Anglo-Americans had such ample supplies of good quality rubber to make tyres like these. But if they did belong to, say, American vehicles, what were they doing out here in this remote wilderness? But there seemed no answer he could find to that overwhelming question. So in the end, he returned to the camp and without a word to a still-awake Brandt, who was proving to be an excellent adjutant, he snuggled inside the comforting warmth of his sleeping bag, telling himself that the morrow was going to be another hard slog, so why worry about matters that he couldn't explain? Within minutes he was fast asleep...

Djebel Lessouda, Eastern Dorsa, Tunisia, Night of Jan 22nd–23rd 1943

'Wheels,' Jenkins told himself as he crouched there in the darkness, observing the camp of US First Armored Division below. It was already very dark. But the camp appeared to be wide awake. It wasn't just the usual sentries, but the tankers themselves. Some were wandering round aimlessly. Others were in groups, slinging horseshoes for money in what light from the camp fires they could find. A few just stood there, staring out into the dark waste, as if they could see things there unseen by their comrades.

In spite of his problems, Jenkins, the deserter-murderer, gave one of his cynical, knowing smiles. He could guess what the tankers' problem was. He had seen it before when new units had arrived on the Russian front, when he had served there with the regular forces of the *Wehrmacht*. Those guys down there were greenhorns, new to combat. Although they might well be dog tired, they weren't able to sleep because they were jumpy and nervous. He guessed they'd be seeing a Kraut in every shadow and piece of camel thorn that waved in the cold night breeze.

He shivered and realized just how cold he was, too. It was high time he got himself some wheels and heat. Although he had been born in poor conditions in Germany, as a kid immigrant he had soon gotten used to American 'luxury', as he saw it. Steam heat and an automobile had quickly became his main wish: one in which he had indulged himself as soon as he had had the where-withal to be able to afford it. Leave the marching and cold to those crackpot kids of the Kraut army, brought up in the tough conditions and discipline of the Hitler Youth. 'Fast as a greyhound, tough as leather, hard as Krupp steel,' they had boasted. He smirked again. Well, let the silly bastards have the lot. He, Hermann Joe Jenkins wanted comfort in the shape of wheels.

On the face of it, his plan was simple. He'd get down into the Yankee outfit's transport lines, line up a jeep, push it noiselessly to the edge of the Djebel, jump behind the steering wheel and ride silently away down the incline before starting the motor. With a bit of luck, he might find some duds in the vehicle – the Yanks were notoriously careless with their gear – perhaps a pair of US military overalls. He could dump his German uniform then, and bluff his way through any Yank checkpoint he might encounter during the second half of his plan. With a bit of luck, he'd be on the boat back to the States, once the Intelligence guys had checked him out, before January was over. But first, he had to get his wheels, despite the GIs moving about all over the place, as if they had gotten ants in their pants. Still, he consoled himself. Even now, dressed in German uniform as he was, he'd be able to fool any Yank that stopped him and didn't see the tell-tale *Wehrmacht* tunic, his accent was so good, almost perfect, even if he did say so himself.

His mind made up, he started to move towards the camp, crouched low, a sock filled with sand, his only weapon, but one he wouldn't hesitate to use if the worst came to the worst.

Like a great predatory cat, Jenkins slunk down, moving quietly for such a big, broad man. On all sides he heard the sentries calling out the code-word challenge at every suspicious shadow: *'Snafu?'* He gave a grin. He did not need to strain for the counter-sign; he could guess it. It would be the GI translation of the original challenge – *'Situation Normal All Fucked Up'*, or perhaps something less profane, *'You're damned right'*. Not that he was going to answer any challenge. He would act first, and that would be that.

Slowly he wandered down a line of silent Sherman tanks, the first he had seen.

They stood, dripping miserably in the drizzle. For several moments he crouched, staring at the metal monsters, considering one of the thirty-ton tanks as possible 'wheels'. But then he dismissed them. They'd be too complicated for him, though he had driven a German Mark III panzer in Russia. He passed on.

A line of artillery shells, covered by tarpaulin, well spread out in heaps to prevent a mass explosion. No good for him. He crept closer to the main camp. From somewhere he could hear a gramophone playing a scratchy record of 'The Boogie-Woogie Bugle Boy of Company B'. 'Nigger music,' he whispered scornfully to himself, as he rounded a big supply tent and stopped dead.

They were the exact thing. Just his collar size, as the Krauts said. Jeeps perhaps half a dozen of them. As he reached out to touch the bonnet of the nearest one, which was still warm, he realized that they had been used recently. With a bit of luck, no one would have attempted to immobilize them yet. Perhaps the little runarounds were used by messengers or the like and would be in use again soon. He hoped so.

Now he gripped the sand-filled sock more tightly – just in case. He'd try to take one close to the edge of the circle of vehicles. That way he'd be closer to the getaway spot. He licked his suddenly parched lips. 'Jesus Christ,' he said to himself in English, 'I'd give my right ball for a good stiff shot of rye at this moment.' Then he forgot the drink and concentrated on the jeep that he considered would be ideal for his purpose. He touched the hood. It was very hot. Good. That meant it might well not be immobilized. It also meant, though he did not take that into account at that moment, that whoever had left without immobilizing it might well be making an appearance at any moment to make use of the vehicle.

Cautiously, he crept into the seat and fumbled in the glowing darkness with the controls, noting as he did so that there was a jeep coat flung over the other seat. With luck, he told himself, there might be some documents in one of its pockets that might give him enough ID to fool anyone trying to check him.

He licked his lips once again. It was now or never. Despite the biting night cold, he felt his body break out in sweat with tension. If he had got it wrong, he knew, he wouldn't stand a chance. The Yank sentries were pretty close. He could see the glowing red ends of their cigarettes only metres away as they patrolled back and forth. 'Piss or get off the frigging pot, buddy,' he commanded himself harshly.

The next instant he started the jeep. A whine. A throaty, reluctant cough. He felt the drops of sweat trickling down the small of his back unpleasantly. With a roar, the engine burst into full life. Petrol stench flooded the air. He thrust home first gear. There was no time for subterfuge now. 'Hey buddy,' an angry voice cried. 'What are you doing with my frigging jeep?'

He didn't answer. He had other things to do. Instead, he released the brake. The jeep started to roll forward towards the slope that led from the hilltop US camp. A figure clad only in long johns and a helmet rushed out of one of the tents. 'What the damned Sam Hill's going on,' he demanded.

Jenkins raced towards him.

'Hey, stop that!' The GI in the long johns extended his arms like a schoolkid playing a catch-and-stop game. Jenkins didn't hesitate. He crashed into him. The man disappeared beneath the jeep's wheels, yelling in agony as he did so. Moments later Jenkins was racing down the hill into the darkness, with scarlet flame and angry yells following him purposelessly. He'd done it. He had his 'wheels'.

He laughed out loud as the wind rustled his hair, and behind him the shooting died away. He whooped like one of the Indians he remembered from the cowboy movies of his childhood and yelled exuberantly, *'Look out America – here I come!'*

Happy Valley HQ, Jan 23rd 1943

The reports, signalled as 'top priority' and 'top secret' with the express permission of the Supreme Commander General Eisenhower himself, had been coming into Nichols's office at Fredendall's headquarters almost hourly now. For at least two days, the boffins at far-off Bletchley in the English Home Counties had been working all-out, deciphering the products of the Enigma signals passing between Hitler's HQ in the East and von Arnim's and Rommel's.

Time and time again, Nichols had whispered to himself, as if afraid to disclose the top secret messages aloud in case someone overheard his monologues. 'Yes, that's another one ... Massing of German fighters ... Tenth German Panzer on the move ... Oh yes. The balloon's going up soon, that's for certain.' Twice he had tried to make an appointment with the Second Corps Commander to reveal his findings; twice he had been turned down, with 'the CG's too busy to deal with Intelligence at this moment in time.' Once, indeed, he had overheard the staff officer in question sneer, 'It's that Limey fag, General. He's a real nervous nelly, that guy. He says the Krauts are coming.' He had been unable to hear Fredendall's reply, but he could guess what it might well have been. 'Doesn't that Limey realize I've got more important things to do than frig around with his goddam Intelligence games ... I've got an HQ to build.'

Because the General wouldn't see him, he had taken up the Ultra signal that German tanks were on the move to below the Faid Pass with Fredendall's chief-of-staff. But the bespectacled Colonel, who looked more like a Mid-Western small-town banker than a regular army officer, had pooh-poohed the top secret signal. 'How the Sam Hill can some guy in England know that the Krauts are moving tanks over here in Africa?' he had snorted, his fat jowls wobbling in angry disbelief.

The American hadn't been initiated into the 'Ultra' secret, so Nichols couldn't tell him where the information had come from. All he could say was, 'Colonel, you may take it as gospel that this is top-level, totally accurate information.' He allowed himself a little joke. 'Why, it could have come from the pen of Field Marshal Rommel himself,' which was probably true. But as always with the Americans, irony was wasted. The fat colonel said, 'I don't care if it came from the Good Lord himself, I just don't believe it.' And that was that.

Nichols, well aware that a crisis was looming – how great he didn't know at that moment – felt totally blocked and frustrated. He knew he had the Supreme Commander's ear and, to a certain extent, his authority, too. But US military procedure and custom frowned upon a senior commander giving more than just advice to a subordinate general except in a real emergency. Eisenhower, he guessed, would abide by that unspoken rule too. So in heaven's name, how was he going to convince Fredendall of the urgency of this German build-up on his front?

As he confided to the 'Cherrypicker', who knew most of his secrets and acted as his sounding board, 'It could make a bloke pull his hair out, well, if I had the kind of flowing un-military locks you have, Sarge.' He smiled and once again admired the 'Cherry-picker's' fine head of over-long hair, something which had first attracted him to the young soldier.

'These things are sent to try us, Colonel,' the latter said with a mock sigh and a quick look upwards, as if appealing to God himself. 'I mean, Old Jerry's got his Eyeties, we've got the Yanks.'

Nichols forced a grin. 'Suppose so. But don't express that kind of sentiment too loud. Remember, they're all around us down here. Damn the bloody place.'

They both laughed shortly and got down to work once again.

That afternoon Fredendall relented somewhat. He sent out a patrol from one of his armoured battalions to check for enemy activity which Ultra had reported in the Faid Pass area. He called Nichols into his underground office to tell him what the patrol had radioed back. '*Nothing*,' he snapped, 'absolutely nothing. In addition, Colonel Water's men report that – and I quote – "area impossible for armoured vehicles, theirs or ours".'

Nichols objected. 'But, sir, German reports indicate that their own armoured engineers are working flat out to regrade the trail leading up to the Pass for use by armour.'

'Bullshit!' Fredendall interrupted him crudely. 'Colonel Waters, the commander of the armoured battalion, is the son-in-law of General George S.Patton—'

Nichols nodded, as if he had heard of this American general, though in reality, he had no idea who he was, though Fredendall had made him seem important.

'—Waters is a West Pointer and a very serious young officer – Patton wouldn't have let *his* daughter marry someone who wasn't going far in the US Army.' Fredendall laughed shortly and Nichols said, 'Yes. I suppose it does help, though, in the promotion stakes, to be married to the general's daughter,' but as before, irony was wasted on Fredendall.

'So in conclusion, you can rely one hundred per cent on Waters's report. There are no Krauts up there,' the US general said.

'Did this Colonel Waters go up there and check personally, sir?' Nichols ventured.

'God Almighty, how should I know? All I know is that he says there are no Krauts near the Faid Pass and I take his word for it. That's all, Colonel.' He was dismissed and had achieved nothing, absolutely nothing at all.

Nichols returned to his own cave, which was vibrating with yet another round of high explosive blasting, followed by the ear-splitting rattle of the US engineers' jackhammers, an angry and sorely troubled man. It seemed to him at that moment, he'd need to work a bloody miracle to save the Yanks from themselves...

The Faid Pass, Jan 24th 1943

Jenkins was a happy man. His gut was full, and he had even bummed a shot of booze from the black who had picked him up after the stolen jeep had run out of gas. Although he was no real redneck, he'd didn't like blacks. He agreed with the Nazis and a goodly number of American Southerners that they were an inferior race, just good enough to haul supplies, bury 'stiffs' and, if they were really intelligent, which most of them weren't, drive two-and-a-half ton trucks as his benefactor Washington Lee did.

Now, as they rolled up the slope towards where Colonel Waters's tank battalion of the First US Armored Division was dug in, Jenkins felt he was almost home and dry. For a while as they had driven towards the high pass, he considered whether he should clout Washington Lee over his thick skull and steal his ID. But he had decided that wasn't the best of plans. What would he do with a black man's pass? Besides, everyone knew just how tough their skulls were – look how Max Schmeling had hammered the 'Brown Bomber' Joe Louis before the war and how the black boxer had still beaten him. No, that wasn't the answer.

Still, with his stomach now full, a shot of booze inside of him, wearing an American overall and coming into the camp in an American truck, no one was going to query him. Once established in the place, he'd look for some real ID and a uniform to allow him to continue the last phase of his journey in safety, and then back to the good ole US of A. For he had read in the German Army magazine, *Signal*, that the Yanks sent their escaped POWs back home so that they didn't have to serve on the front where they had been captured a second time. At the time, he had complained to his fellow Brandenburgers, 'What a bunch of frigging asparagus Tarzans those *Amis* are. Could you see the German Army doing that, comrades?' They couldn't. Now he was very damned glad that the US Army was that soft and made up of 'asparagus Tarzans'.

Five minutes later, a suddenly nervous Washington Lee was obviously worried about being in the presence of so many white men. 'Whiteys' were moody folk; a black man, who wanted to avoid having his head kicked in, had to watch them all the time.

He dropped Jenkins off, with 'Many thanks for your company, Cap'n.'

Lifting Lee's last pack of Camels from the pocket of his 'Ike' jacket, Jenkins waved and said, 'Think nothing of it, *boy.*'

A few minutes later, Jenkins casually joined the main chow-line. He picked up somebody's canteen and canteen cup, and shuffled forward with rest of the GIs to where a group of cooks in dirty singlets, wreathed in steam from the great open pans, were dishing out their wares. Jenkins was not particularly hungry, but he knew anyone eating out of a GI canteen wouldn't be thought suspect, and the long wait in line would give him time to check the camp out.

'Kay, you guys,' the head cook, fat, sweating face heavy with an unshaven beard, was crying. 'You've got two choices, you lucky stiffs. There's beans 'n' franks, or today's special – shit on shingle.' He guffawed as a moan went up from the GIs. 'Jesus H. Sarge, not frigging chipped beef on toast again?'

'Blow it outta yer barracks bag,' the big cook replied unfeelingly. 'Or go and take your tough shit chit to the chaplain, guys.' He turned and ordered his staff, ''Kay, you guys start dishing up, while I go to my private dining room and eat a couple of rare steaks.'

His supposed witticism fell flat. The GIs were not in a mood for jokes. Like beaten animals, shoulders hunched, they held out their canteens for the 'shit on shingle' and the customary 'beans 'n' franks' with hardly another complaint. Jenkins told himself they looked a lot of sad sacks. The *Wehrmacht* would eat them alive if they ever attacked in this direction.

Jenkins forgot the chow. He stared around the camp as he spooned down luke-warm beans. Over to the left, there were the officers' quarters. He could see that from the smaller two-man tents with smoke curling from the tin chimneys in their roofs. Officers had heat; enlisted men didn't. He decided that wasn't the place to look for what he sought. Then he had it. Larger tents, probably intended to hold more than a platoon. There, men could come and go without anyone asking questions of them.

He ate the last of the beans, ignoring the cheap frankfurters which had obviously been taken from their cans and dunked for a couple of minutes in luke-warm water, and dropping the canteen next to the washtub without attempting to clean it, sauntered apparently casually to the nearest large tent. He paused at the opening and made a fuss of lighting one of Washington Lee's Camels. No one seemed to be inside. He cocked his head to one side and listened intently. Nothing. The place was empty.

He tapped his pocket, in which he had hidden the home-made blackjack. It was now or never. He pushed the flap to one side, to be greeted by the normal soldiers' fug, a mixture of cheap tobacco and sweaty feet. He went inside. The place was a mess, a German sergeant's nightmare. There were weapons everywhere, with piles of junk, half-eaten Hershey bars and open copies of *Stars & Stripes*, the soldiers' newspaper, on the unmade bunks, and – Jenkins's eyes sparkled – jackets and other bits of clothing hanging from the tent poles on all sides.

Now he knew there was no time to be wasted. Someone might come in and catch him at any moment. Deftly, he ran his big hands down jackets and trench coats, searching for ID cards or wallets that might contain them. Now his nerves were jingling electrically with tension. 'Come on for Chrissake,' he hissed to himself urgently. 'Where the frig are you?'

He found out. Well, it felt like it. A stiff shape in the upper pocket of a T/5, to judge by the stripes and insignia, of some technical specialist or so. Jenkins didn't concern himself with the man's rank or trade. With fumbling, nervous fingers that felt at that particular moment like clumsy pork sausages, he fought open the stiff jacket button. He gave a swift smile of triumph and reached in the pocket in the very same moment that a thin, reedy voice demanded angrily, 'say buddy, what ya doing in my jacket?'

Jenkins turned, startled.

A small, bespectacled man stood there, fists clenched angrily. For a moment, Jenkins was at a loss for words. He recovered swiftly. Taking the measure of the man, who looked like some company clerk, and telling himself he could fell him with one hand tied behind his back, he said, 'what d'ya mean?'

Surprisingly enough, the little man didn't seem afraid of Jenkins's bulk and big fists. He snorted, 'Too much of this goddam thieving going on. I've a good mind to turn you in you thieving bastard.'

Jenkins saw his danger. The man could turn and shout the alarm through the tent's opening and then, as the Krauts said, 'the tick-tock would really be in the pisspot'. He changed his tone immediately. He wheedled, lowering his bull-like head to hide the murder in his eyes, 'Don't get me wrong, pal ... I was just looking for a butt. Come on over here and I'll show ya.'

A little puzzled, wondering now if he had made a mistake, the little man wound his way through the bunks to where Jenkins stood, looking very humble and contrite, if that was possible in his case. 'But I don't have no butts,' the man said. 'I don't smoke. Besides, the company commander would allow me—' He stopped short. For the first time, he saw the pass in Jenkins's hand. 'Hey, guy,' he exclaimed, his anger returning, 'what the hell are you doing with my ID?'

Jenkins didn't answer. Instead, he lashed out with his big right fist. He missed striking the other man's weak jaw as he had intended. He merely struck his shoulder. The blow sent him reeling backwards and he didn't go down. Instead, he slammed against one of the bunks, steadied himself and yelled at the top of his voice, 'Guys, there's something funny going on over here ... Olsen, Jones, come and give me a hand. Some bastard's trying to rob me!'

Jenkins panicked. Outside, there came cries and the sounds of running feet. The man's friends and tent-mates were coming to help him. He had to make a run for it. Wildly, he flung a glance to left and right. He couldn't go out the way he'd entered. He'd run straight into the arms of the little swine's pals. The rear entrance? Yes, that was the way out.

'Stay where you are,' the little man commanded. Somewhere he'd found a wrench.

Recovered from Jenkins's blow, he was advancing on the German-American with the tool raised above his head – and it looked as if he was prepared to use it.

Jenkins didn't wait for him to try. He turned and sprang over the nearest bunk, dropping the precious ID as he did so. There was no time to worry about that now. He fumbled with the laces of the canvas at the back of the big tent. To his rear, a big man armed with a pistol thrust open the flap and fired. The slug tore a burning hole in the tent wall, only millimetres away from where Jenkins fumbled to undo the laces. 'Hold it, buddy!' the big man commanded.

Jenkins wasn't listening. He knew instinctively that the man with the pistol wouldn't shoot him in cold blood in the back. *Amis* were too soft to do that.

With a gasp, he flung open the last of the laces. 'I said hold it—' the man with the gun repeated, but already Jenkins was through, then running for his life down the slope and away from the camp on the pass. But even as he ran, arms working like pistons, going all-out, he knew he'd fucked it up. Now he was really in a mess...

THE BETRAYAL

'March or croak.'
Old German Army Saying

The Devil's Garden, Feb First 1943

'Look, sir,' Brandt said thickly. They had been on half rations of water for the last forty-eight hours and were parched. Most of them found it difficult to speak, they were so dry. 'I think I can see vehicles.'

Scharf, as parched as the young officer, peered through the early morning gloom. He guessed that Brandt might be right. They should be about through the 'Devil's Garden' by now. The route had been tough, very tough, and somehow he doubted if Rommel's tankers could make it and make the surprise flank attack, which the Field Marshal hoped would turn the American front in south-west Tunisia. Still, if those trucks over there, stark black outlines against the grey-flushing dawn sky, could, perhaps Rommel's panzers might do so also. Anyway, it was worth looking at.

He turned to the one-armed officer crouched next to him in the scrub and whispered – for he knew just how far voices carried in the silence of the desert at dawn.

'Whistle up Hartmann and a couple of his thugs. I'm going to have a look-see.'

Brandt looked a little peeved. 'You don't want me, sir.' Inadvertently he glanced at his missing arm, as if blaming it for everything.

'Brandt, not at this moment. Mind you,' he consoled the other officer, 'if yours truly runs into trouble, you'll be in charge of the whole show. Now let's move it ... *dalli* ... *dalli*.'

Brandt moved it *'dalli ... dalli'*. A few minutes later, Scharf, pistol already drawn, accompanied by the ex-legionnaire and a couple of his 'old hares', was creeping forward to the silent trucks; they could already smell the tantalizing odour of frying bacon, so they guessed that someone was up and awake in the little desert laager.

They crawled through some prickly camel scrub and paused at the edge, still concealed in the stuff. Here they surveyed the little encampment. They used the old Brandenburger desert trick to obtain better vision: they swung their heads to one side as far as they could, then turned their gaze slowly to their front. A moment's pause. Then everything came, for some reason or other, into clear perspective. Now they could make out the details of the little camp more clearly.

There were three trucks formed into a rough circle. On the ground near a dying fire of camel scrub, dark shapes were lying, wrapped in blankets, men presumably still asleep. Next to them, blowing every now and again to keep the camel fire flaming, a fat man in a stocking cap was crouching frying what was obviously bacon in a large pan. On the fire itself, a pot was giving off the delicious odour of early morning coffee.

Hartmann licked his lips. 'Real bean coffee, sir,' he whispered hoarsely. 'None of that ersatz shit that we've got to drink.'

'Shut up,' Scharf whispered back. 'I can't hear myself thinking.' For the *Oberleutnant* was thinking hard. The men below were obviously *Amis*. But what were *Amis* doing out here in this wasteland? Surely the Americans hadn't established troops here, so far away from their major defences? If they had, he had to look into it. If Rommel were to use this route for his feint or flanking attack, he wouldn't want his panzers to bump into unexpected resistance. He made a quick decision.

'Hartmann, you chowhound, how would you like to sample that *real bean coffee*?'

Hartmann gave him a big, unshaven grin. 'Lead me to it, sir!'

'Right, this is what we're going to do ... and remember that although those fellows down there might be a shower of shit in your opinion, they are armed. So play it careful. I don't want casualties at this stage of the game, clear? Keep your eyes peeled.'

'Sir. I will. Like the proverbial tinned tomatoes,' Hartmann added cheekily. Then he was gone, followed by his two 'old hares', who didn't seem in any way fazed by the thought of just three of them attacking an enemy encampment.

Five minutes later the three of them, moving very quietly for such big, heavy-set men, were in among the still sleeping Americans, the cook at his fire whistling happily as if he hadn't a care in the world – and he had plenty as from that moment, though he didn't know it.

'Left of second truck,' Hartmann hissed, 'sentry ... Fast asleep. Otto, nobble him.'

The old hare needed no urging. Soon the smell of frying bacon and good coffee would waken the men; all soldiers were born chow-hounds. The sooner he dealt with the lone soldier, the better. He moved off, keeping low, his trench knife close to his hip, like a dentist about to extract a tooth from an anxious patient might conceal his forceps.

He paused in front of the sleeping sentry, perched on a ration box, head thrown back to expose his unshaven throat. It was an ideal position. The old hare gave an evil grin. He raised his trench knife and placed the point close to the snoring man's jugular.

'Shave sir?' he enquired pleasantly, though he doubted if the *Ami* would have spoken German even if he had been awake.

He pressed the point in harder. The sentry woke with a start, letting his rifle fall from his grip as he did so, exclaiming, 'What the Sam Hill's going on—' He stopped abruptly. His eyes widened with terror as he saw the grinning man leering down at him with a knife in his big dirty paw. 'What ... what—' The old hare pressed the point into his throat even harder. The words dried up immediately. Without turning, the old hare whistled softly.

Hartmann and the other Brandenburger came up almost noiselessly. In that same instant, a fat man in his long johns, carrying a wad of paper, came round from behind the second truck. He was obviously heading for the sands to carry out the business of evacuating his bowels. As Hartmann commented crudely after it was all over, 'He didn't need to go that far, comrades. He shat himself on the spot. I saw to that.'

Hartmann fired from the hip without aiming. The fat man in his underwear faltered in mid-stride. For a moment nothing else happened. Suddenly he screamed, almost in outrage and not in pain. He looked down at his stomach. The dirty white of his long johns was beginning to stain a deep red, the stain widening by the second. He looked up at his attacker, as if accusing him. Next moment he flopped to the ground, dead before he hit it.

The fight went out of the rest almost immediately. Within the next five minutes, the attackers had their sullen, frightened prisoners, in various states of undress, squatting on the sandy ground, hands clasped around their necks, while the victors wolfed down hunks of good white bread and greasy bacon, their bearded chins dripping with fat, washing the splendid feast down with drafts of the kind of coffee that most of them had not tasted since before the war.

A satisfied Scharf gave them time to enjoy the meal, savouring the good rich American coffee himself and telling himself that if the *Wehrmacht* could only feed its half-starved troops this kind of food, they'd beat the world. Then he got down to business, using one of the German-Americans, Hofstetter, to translate for him.

The fact that Hofstetter spoke 'American' like they did seemed to put the prisoners at their ease. Yet when it came to questions of what they were doing out here in the middle of nowhere at a place where there was supposed to be no US troops, they were strangely reticent. At first, Scharf thought they were being good soldiers who were refusing to give away military information. But soon he reasoned that was not the case. And they were certainly not good soldiers. Some of them had actually forgotten their military service numbers, and two were without their dog tags. Without dog tags, even the most average soldier usually felt lost.

In the end, with persistent but friendly questioning and cigarettes being handed out to the prisoners all the time – the captors could afford to be generous with the *Amis'* own looted 'cancersticks' – it came out. They were in fact deserters from the enemy's own Second Corps Headquarters, who had gotten lost on their way to Tunis. They had hoped to sell stolen US Army tyres (two of the trucks were filled with them) on the capital's black market, where such goods brought a fortune.

Naturally, they hadn't realized that Tunis was still in German hands. All they had been concerned with was 'selling the goods and getting some dough, sir,' as one of them explained at last, 'so we could whoop it up with the local gals and drink plenty o'good likker.'

Scharf told himself that would be the day. As far as he was concerned – and probably the Yankee 'white mice'* too – they wouldn't

*Nickname for the white-helmeted US military police.

be enjoying the favours of the local whores for many a day to come.

Later when he was alone with Brandt, he considered how to get rid of his prisoners. He had no intention of shooting them in cold blood as Hartmann suggested, for once they were released, if that's what he did with them, they'd present no danger. He could not see them heading for the nearest US outfit to report on their former captors. After all, they were deserters, and thieves to boot.

'I think the best thing is to give 'em a kick up the arse and let 'em go,' he told Brandt after a while. 'And remove their boots too. All *Amis* have poor feet. That'll stop them going off at a gallop.'

Brandt laughed. 'You're right sir. Too much riding about in automobiles. And that fattening meat.'

Scharf joined in his laughter. 'I doubt if they'll be seeing much of that Hamburger meat of theirs in the near future. Now here's what we'll do...'

They set off that night, together with the newly captured deserters' trucks. Now Scharf turned in a south-easterly direction, heading straight for where he knew roughly that the main American positions were. His plan was daring, but he felt he had to take the risks entailed in order to deflect US interest from the 'Devil's Garden' route and confirm their belief that when and if a German attack came, it would be from the other direction.

As they progressed out of the empty waste that even the Arabs avoided, the going got better, so that they arrived roughly in the area where he would make his feint, and he was able to make a brief stop for a drink and a rest and explain to his men what he intended.

Now he gazed around the circle of their bronzed, bearded faces, hollowed out by the privations of the last few days into deaths' heads – even the German-Americans, who by his standards seemed overweight and overfed, had been whittled down by the meagre diet – and liked what he saw. He knew he could rely on these men to hell and back again.

'I won't attempt to fool you, comrades,' he said in a quiet voice. 'You deserve the truth after what you've been through. I'm going to take you close to the *Ami* lines – and I want the *Amis* to see us. I know that can be dangerous. But we must get that close so that their officers report back that a large German patrol has been spotted to their front. Why?'

He answered his own question. 'Because I want the *Amis* to believe that this is where Field Marshal Rommel's attack will come in when it does, so the real attack will catch the *Amis* by complete surprise.'

He paused and let them absorb the information, their faces grave and thoughtful, before adding, 'I know. I know that such matters of higher strategy don't really concern hairy-assed stubble hoppers like ourselves. We're usually too busy trying to ensure that we don't look at the taties from beneath.'

One or two laughed hollowly at the old soldier's expression for being buried. But most of them remained as grave as ever, as if they were considering that out here in this remote waste, their fate, life or death, was being decided.

Just before he was about to order his men to mount up, Scharf decided he'd better 'take a shovel for a walk'. Old soldier that he was, he didn't want a full gut in case he was hit; his chances of survival were better that way. So while his men finished off the last of the delightful looted *Ami* 'real coffee beans' and had a smoke in the cover of the trucks, he left the little circle to carry out what his dead mother had called, when he had been a little boy, his 'duty'.

It was while he was squatting there in the eerie silence of the desert at dawn that his eye fell on a crude frieze cut into the face of the rock opposite. It depicted tall, obviously black warriers fighting other warriors, both lots totally naked and carrying spears. It seemed to be a battle for a waterhole, for in the centre of the frieze there was a recognizable depiction of a palm tree. He smiled softly and finished what he had to do. Eight thousand years old, probably, from when people still lived in this arsehole of the world, he told himself, and they were already fighting each other.

He completed the job and picked up his Schmeisser – they were too close to the *Amis* now. It was better to carry a weapon, even when 'taking a shovel for a walk'. He slipped off the safety catch. There was no time now for fancy philosophical thoughts about the futility of human existence.

Half an hour later, with a wintry sun rising reluctantly over the horizon to the east as if some god on high wondered whether he should illuminate the war-torn world below, they reached a great curved sweep on a perfectly flat plain: perfect tank country. Scharf told himself that it was the sort of terrain that the green *Amis* would expect any attacker with tanks to use. He smiled. But they didn't know the German Army. The *Wehrmacht* never fought conventional battles; they always attempted the unexpected. That was the way to win.

But he was right about the *Amis*. Scharf

focused his field glasses to his immediate front and there they were: neatly spaced out brown gun pits, each one containing those ineffectual enemy 57mm anti-tank guns, whose shells bounced off the thick steel hides of German tanks like glowing ping-pong balls. He nodded, as if coming to a decision. 'Brandt,' he snapped, very businesslike now.

'Sir?'

'This is it. Now we shall start our demonstration of force. And, please me. Don't do anything heroic. Most heroes I've known are long dead.'

Brandt shared his little smile. 'I'll do my best, sir.'

'Good man ... Heaven, arse and cloudburst, follow me, the captain's got a hole in his arse!' Scharf cried exuberantly, carried away yet once again by the wild unreasoning atavatism of battle. Then, well spread out to make the smallest possible targets, they were darting forward across the flat plain, driving all-out, sending up a brown wake of flying sand behind them. This was it.

The American defenders reacted slowly. Even as they hurtled forward, they could see officers and NCOs running back and forth like headless chickens, obviously wondering how they should react. Finally, after what seemed an age, though it may well have been only a matter of minutes, the nearest anti-tank gun belched. A white blur sprang from the long barrel. Next moment it was speeding towards the attackers, keeping a low trajectory. Scharf could have cheered. The greenhorns over there were firing solid anti-tank shells instead of high explosive ones they should have used against thin-skinned vehicles such as theirs. A solid shot shell would just go through their canvas hoods without harm, without even being noticed. They sped on.

Now sweeping across the plain, the Staghound armoured car pumping shells at the defenders, all of them ignoring the shells hissing lethally through their ranks, for the American gunners were still rattling and had not yet changed to HE shells, they headed straight for the defenders' line. Scharf knew from past experience in Russia, if one pressed home a wild attack like this to the hilt, the defenders would break and make a run for it. But the attackers shouldn't suffer casualties. That would put heart into the defenders and make them stick to their guns. If that were the case, he'd break off the attack and run for it. He wasn't going to risk the lives of his brave volunteers more than necessary.

They came closer and closer. Scharf could see the leaders running back and forth bringing more shells, while the gun-aimers peered over the edge of their guns' steel shields, directing their weapons the best they could, trying to penetrate the clouds of flying sand everywhere. Now they were a matter of two hundred metres away. At that range even green, rattled gunners like the *Amis* couldn't miss. Now either they'd score a hit, or they'd break and the day would be Scharf's. But now, his luck ran out.

Suddenly, startlingly, the Staghound armoured car staggered. It reared back on its boogies like some wild horse being put to the saddle for the first time. Next moment it came to a stop. Bright white smoke poured from its open turret. A Brandenburger, already blazing like a torch, flung himself out of the holed turret. For a few seconds, the crewman writhed back and forth in the sand in his agony, greedy blue flames reaching higher and higher up his tortured, charring body. Then he was still.

That first 'kill' seemed to signal a wave of new hope in the American gunners. They blazed away now, firing more accurately. Their shells started landing more closely to the flying vehicles. A looted truck was hit. It slewed to one side, front tyres torn to shreds, trailing burning rubber behind it, men jumping for their lives, knowing that its engine would explode at any moment. It did.

For a moment, it vanished in a geyser of whirling flame and smoke. When it came into view again a few seconds later, it was just a burning ribcage, with the dead, horribly charred driver still poised at his wheel.

A few minutes later, as under Scharf's command the attacking vehicles circled like redskins circling a settlers' convoy in some Wild West movie, the American gunners must have realized they were firing the wrong kind of shell for soft-skinned vehicles. They changed to high explosive. Now, as the Brandenburgers came in again, high explosive began to throw up huge fountains of earth and grass all about their vehicles. In vain, one of the German-Americans tried the old trick. He stood upright in the wildly swaying jeep as it bucked and jerked over the tracks they had made the first time and yelled at the top of his voice, 'Cease firing, guys ... For Chrissake, cease firing, we're Americans!'

Whether or not the American anti-tank gunners heard, they did not cease their assault. Instead, they seemed to intensify their fire. Yet another flying truck was hit. It exploded with a muffled noise. The canvas flew apart and started burning immediately. The tyres which the American deserters had intended to sell on the black market followed rings of burning rubber trailing behind the crippled vehicle till it faltered to a stop.

Scharf realized that it was time to break off the feint. He was losing too many men. Standing upright the best he could, ignoring the shells exploding all around him, he placed his hand on the top of his helmet, fingers outspread. It was the infantry signal for 'close on me'.

His men reacted as one. In a great sweep he turned to the left, his men following. They knew he was leading them away from the fight. The American gunners seemed to know that, too. They pushed their guns out of their pits to get better aims and began firing wildly at the retreating attackers. But their aim was too erratic, and already the first of the Brandenburgers were out of the range of the 57mm cannon, about six hundred metres. Seconds later they were out of range totally, just dark dots on the horizon, hurrying back the way they had come, with a worried Scharf telling himself it wouldn't be long now and, dozy as they were in battle, the *Amis* would have their planes out searching for them. They'd have to get their heads down somewhere before that happened...

Scharf was right. The American planes caught up with the battered little convoy sooner than Scharf had anticipated. Perhaps it was because he had stopped so that they could fill up the tanks of their vehicles to the brim in case they were chased for hours. But then there they were. Two twin-boomed Lightning fighter-planes, the latest American models in the African war theatre.

Scharf cursed and let his binoculars drop to his chest. The *Ami* fighters had spotted them all right. They had decreased speed now, and were beginning to circle in the grey sullen sky like wary hawks. Scharf knew why. They were sizing the little convoy up as it hurried along in clouds of dust, checking whether the vehicles had any anti-aircraft devices. They hadn't. Now they prepared to crush these intruders like some giant might crush inferior beetles scuttling along the floor underfoot without a single further thought.

Brandt looked at him. He shook his head. There was no answer to the one-armed officer's unspoken question. Now their fate was in the hands of the gods. He tried to grin. 'Thank God for what we are about to receive,' he intoned with mock piety like some feeble priest, 'and make sure we make handsome car—' He never finished the old hare's cynical saying.

With startling suddenness the first Lightning dropped out of the sky. At over four hundred kilometres an hour, it flashed across the surface of featureless plain, its prop-wash thrashing the camel thorn to and fro. To a transfixed Scharf, the plane seemed to fill the whole horizon. He could see the pilot behind his glazed dome in detail now. He could even make out that he was wearing sunglasses, for some reason or other. But he had no further time to dwell on that little puzzle. The plane was almost on them now. It deafened him with the roar of its engines.

Next moment, the American opened fire. The rattle and clatter of slugs was terrific. 20mm cannon shells hissed towards the fleeing trucks like a swarm of angry bees. All around them, the ground erupted in vicious little spurts. Up front, their driver yelped with pain; blood spurted from his shoulder in a bright-red glittering arc. 'It's all right, sir,' he cried, as Scharf attempted to help him. 'I've had worse knocks in bar-room battles in Bremen.'

'Good man,' Scharf bellowed as the Lightning, its first run complete, overshot the fleeing convoy and zoomed high into the sky, leaving a bright white trail behind him. Scharf wiped the beads of sweat from his forehead and told himself: the *Ami* might have missed. His wing man wouldn't. For behind them, the other pilot, also flying at ground height, had lowered his flaps and feathered back his engine. It was almost as if he wished to stall. But the battle-experienced Major knew that was not the *Ami*'s aim.

He was steadying his plane to make it the most perfect possible platform for launching his attack. *He* was not going to overshoot the convoy without a fatal hit as his leader had done. He was coming in for the kill...

Second Corps Intelligence Headquarters, Feb 2nd 1943

'My name is Jenkins, sir, Private First Class Ray Jenkins,' the prisoner lied glibly. Since his capture, he had regained his confidence. The Yanks had helped. They had treated him like a common thief. A couple of the big, hulking 'white mice' had knocked him about a bit, calling him a 'sneaking, thieving bastard...'

'Holy smoke,' one of them had exploded in indignation, 'What kind of a jerk are you – stealing from a buddy like that.' He had slapped Jenkins across his unshaven face, rocking his head from side to side.

All the same, no one had attempted to find out why he was a 'sneaking, thieving bastard'. After all, what use were greenbacks in this goddam desert? There was nothing to buy with goddam folding money. So, confidence restored, Jenkins decided he was safe. He could play it his way. The only problem was that he had no ID.

The captain of US Military Intelligence

interrogating Jenkins after he had been handed over by the MPs who had arrested him at the pass looked up from his file and said, 'Where are your dog tags, Jenkins? You know a soldier has got to keep them on his person all the time.'

Jenkins was ready for that question at least. He stared down at the little Yid, barely able to conceal his contempt for the 'Hebe', who thought he was so damned smart. 'Left them on my bunk, sir. The metal chain that holds them gave me some kind of a rash. The MO said it was to do with excessive sweating out here. Told me to keep them off for a few days and it'd go away.' Even before the Jew could ask the next question, which he anticipated, Jenkins said, 'I had a slip from the medics, sir. But I kinda lost it.' He did his best to look humble and foolish like some typical sad sack of a GI.

Sitting in the shadows at the rear end of the Intelligence tent, 'Crasher' Nichols frowned. The prisoner, big, hulking and tough-looking, didn't look like the type who would ever feel humble, or forget something, for that matter. But it wasn't merely the prisoner's manner that disconcerted him, it was his accent. As far as he was concerned, Jenkins seemed to speak perfect American English, yet the accent didn't ring quite true. He might be one of those foreign-born Americans, he told himself, and there were plenty of them in the US Army overseas. But his name, Welsh, and his big, broad, Northern European appearance made it quite clear that Jenkins or his forefathers didn't come from Eastern Europe or the Balkans, or somewhere like that.

In what seemed another age now when he had been a don, he used to play a game with his post-graduate students. He'd play them records he had made himself when he, too, had been a post-graduate student, of various German regional accents. They had ranged from the curious medieval German 'Seven Mountain Saxons', peasants who had emigrated to Rumania, Hungary and the like in the Middle Ages, to the sharp, clipped German of the people of the *'waterkant'*, the 'waterfront' of the Baltic and the North Sea. Then it had been up to his students to make an educated guess from whence the speaker had come.

Later he had used his own specialized knowledge of German accents to identify the home areas of German POWs, captured by Monty's Eighth Army. That kind of identification had enabled Nichols to impress on the prisoner that he knew everything about him, even to what town he had originally hailed from. Superiority had been the name of the game in the interrogation of prisoners, especially with Germans, who often thought that the fabled 'English Secret Service', as they called it, were everywhere, spying out every nook and cranny of their German homeland.

Now as he listened to what he had originally taken to be a routine interrogation of some supposed GI who had no real identification and had been caught stealing from a comrade, he was struck by the slight strangeness of Jenkins's speech. For one thing, Jenkins had some difficulty with his 'r's, as many Germans did. He didn't get involved sentence structures quite right either.

Nichols frowned, puzzled, and wondered whether he should intervene or go back to his own tent and signal his superiors that he had done all he could at Second Corps HQ; General Fredendall was simply taking no notice of any warning of the impending attack that he might give.

His thoughts drifted. Behind him, standing at his camp stool, the 'Cherrypicker' stirred, changing from one foot to the other, as if he were bored with the whole business. His hand, surprisingly sensitive for his kind, lay on the edge of Nichols's chair. For one crazy moment Nichols was seized by a wild desire to take it, raise it to his lips and kiss it with all the love that was pent up inside his skinny frame. He caught himself just in time, in the same moment that Jenkins was saying, 'Eventually I shall find my papers sir—'

Nichols sat up abruptly. *'Eventually'*; it was a totally wrong use of the word. Only a German would use it like that. Jenkins was translating directly – and incorrectly – from the German *'eventuell'*, which meant something slightly different. His doubts about the prisoner were justified.

'Captain,' he snapped, breaking into the interrogation. 'Have the prisoner stripped naked.'

The captain shot him a look through his steel-rimmed GI glasses as if he had abruptly gone mad. 'What did you say, sir?'

Nichols repeated his order.

The captain looked aghast. 'But we can't do that, sir. This isn't the NYPD. We don't use third degree methods here, sir.'

Nichols hadn't the foggiest notion what the 'NYPD' was, but he did understand the Captain's reference. The American thought he was going to have Jenkins stripped to humiliate him. It was an old technique; a man who was concerned about what another man thought of his private parts when he was being scrutinized buck-naked by clothed interrogators would soon give in and spill the beans to end all the embarrassment. 'No, Captain, it's not what you think. I'm not about to degrade Jenkins. I'm just trying to ascertain that he's what he purports to be – a thief without proof of identity. Now let us not waste any more time. Get on with it.'

Puzzled, but with his honour satisfied, the officer snapped out an order to the two burly MPs guarding their prisoner. Jenkins reacted angrily. 'Hey, you guys, knock it off, willya? What do you think I am – a goddam Dillinger or something, eh?'

'Just get them duds off,' the bigger of the two military policemen answered. ''Kay?'

The other grabbed Jenkins by the neck and jerked his head back cruelly. The prisoner flushed a beetroot red immediately. 'For Chrissake,' he gasped, 'ya choking me.'

'Shut up!' the MP holding him snarled. He nodded to the other man, who didn't hesitate. He pulled open the prisoner's belt and jerked down his pants. His jacket and undershirt followed, so that in seconds, he was standing there gasping and angry, naked, with his trousers wrapped around his boots.

Nichols went to work at once, guarded by the 'Cherrypicker', who disliked Americans immensely, especially on account of the comments they made about his long blond hair and handsome face. 'Stand up straight when the officer examines you and no messing about – or else, mate.' He clenched his fist significantly.

Nichols smiled a little awkwardly. The

presence of other naked men always embarrassed him. It had as far back as his prep school, when they had been forced to take cold showers after 'games'. He didn't know why, exactly. He guessed it was something to do with his suppressed homosexuality. Now he kept his distance as he examined Jenkins's naked body minutely. The others looked on, puzzled, until the 'Cherrypicker' explained over his shoulder, 'The colonel's looking for any signs of a parachute harness.'

The captain with the steel glasses understood at once. He whistled softly. 'You mean, the colonel thinks he might be an *agent* dropped by parachute?'

The 'Cherrypicker' didn't comment any further. He was watching Jenkins and then Nichols too intently. The boss had to be protected.

Nichols finished with Jenkins's brawny chest: it was strangely pale for someone who had spent time in North Africa, but showed no sign of redness of the chaffing made by a harness. 'Open your legs.'

'Fuck you!' Jenkins cursed and gasped the next moment, as the bigger MP poked his club hard against Jenkins's ribs. Jenkins did as he was ordered. Nichols bent his head closer to Jenkins's loins, smelling the warm, heady odour of male sexuality. He tried to avoid looking at Jenkins's dangling penis, circumcised like most Americans'.

Jenkins looked down at him and said in that sneering, defiant manner of his, 'Like to take a bite, Colonel—'

He never finished. The 'Cherrypicker' hit him very hard. He stumbled back, blood seeping from a suddenly split lip, as the little captain rose from his blanket-covered trestle desk, crying, 'You can't do that sort of thing!' and Nichols himself said in triumph. 'Just take a look at the tattoo underneath his right arm. What do you make of that, Captain?'

Jenkins righted himself with difficulty, the blood pouring from his lip, which was already swelling now, as Nichols ordered, 'Keep that arm, Jenkins, where it is ... up!'

Jenkins obeyed, and Nichols turned to the American Intelligence Officer and asked, 'Ever seen anything like that tattoo before? You should have, really.'

The man looked puzzled. 'I can't ... can't say I have, Colonel,' he answered, staring at the tattoo, which appeared to be a replica of some sort of triangular badge or the like.

'The swastika ... New York's Germantown,' Nichols prompted.

'Holy smoke,' the captain cried, half-rising from his desk again. 'I'm a New Yorker and Jewish too, of course I've seen it before. It's the emblem of Fritz Kuehn's – or whatever the guy's name was – German-American *Bund*. But what ... what's this guy carrying it for?'

'We'll soon find out,' Nichols said purposefully, adding for the sake of the others present, 'Kuehn ran a Nazi organization in the States supported by secret German funds. He was particularly active in New York with a large Jewish pop—'

'Goddam hebes,' Jenkins snarled.

The 'Cherrypicker' hit him again. The sneer vanished as if by magic as he whined, 'There was no need to go and do that. It's a free country. Guy's got a right to his opinions.'

Nichols shook his head in mock wonder. If the situation wasn't so urgent, Jenkins would have made it laughable: the anti-Semitic ex-Nazi talking about a 'free country'.

'All right,' he started on the prisoner right away, 'I'm not going to play games with you, Jenkins. You'd better realize from the very start that your life is forfeit if you don't co-operate with me. I'm going to ask you some questions and I want the answer P.D.Q... . and remember, you are either a traitor or a spy dressed in Allied uniform. I could have you put against the nearest wall and shot right now – without trial. Think of that.'

The Jewish captain looked aghast at the words 'without trial'. In the USA you didn't do that kind of thing, but he told himself that desperate situations needed desperate solutions, so he nodded his head as if he agreed with the effeminate-looking Britisher's every word.

'Here we go,' Nichols said. 'Now, how did you get here and where did you come from, and no lying—'

But Jenkins's spirit was broken now. He couldn't lie any longer. He knew his life was at stake; he had to spill the beans. 'We came from the coast, sir,' he commenced.

'Who's we?'

'A German outfit.'

Nichols made a wild guess. 'Regiment Brandenburg?' he asked hastily.

Jenkins nodded, wondering how much else the little Limey knew – the fag bastard.

'And your mission?'

Jenkins told him what he knew, and now the dam burst and he kept on and on ... while Nichols's mind raced electrically. Jenkins's story unfolded, and the colonel told himself that now Fredendall would have to listen to him. It was the Brandenburgers' probing attack on the Indian brigade on Monty's Mareth Line all over again. This time, however, if the Yanks didn't buck up mightily, a follow-up assault on Second Corps positions could spell nothing but total, absolute disaster...

The Devil's Garden, North Of Gafsa, Feb 3rd 1943

Scharf took the bottle of *Strega* from the fat, drunken Italian officer and took a mighty swig. He needed it. His nerves were still jangling from the near-disaster. He gave a little shudder of pleasure as the fierce Italian liqueur slammed into the back of his throat and trickled red-hot down his gullet.

The fat officer, who was carrying a sword that was much too long for him, beamed with pleasure. '*Prego*,' he said in a thick, rasping, drinker's voice. '*Molto bene, si?*' and then in broken German, 'I get more.' He turned, swayed and almost fell over. Then, with the feathers of the Bersagliere hat he wore drooping as if he were bearing a soaked parrot on his shoulder, he stamped away, bringing each foot down hard as if he were crushing something underfoot, muttering something about 'damned rats ... every-where.' He headed for the little Italian convoy where the whores from the mobile brothel unit were hanging out their knickers to dry on the barrels of the quadruple flak cannon which had saved the Brandenbur-gers' bacon.

Scharf lowered the bottle and gasped for breath, then smiled at his men, who were sampling the brothel's supply of *Peroni* beer, gazing longingly at the Italian whores as they did so, especially the one they called Adriana, the big dyed blonde, who was naked to the waist, her breats like overripe melons as she hung her one and only bra to dry on one of the flak cannon's barrels. Hartmann, holding his bottle of Italian beer as if he might crush it to glass splinters with suppressed passion, was muttering, 'Holy strawsack, comrades, just feast your glassy orbits on them tits ... All that meat and no frigging tatties!'

Scharf smiled his approval. He would be eternally grateful to the Macaronis, the captain with hallucinations who thought he was walking on rats all the time, purple ones at that, the flak gunner deserter with his cannon, who acted as the mobile brothel's 'chucker-out', and the whores, even Adriana, she of the enormous naked breasts. If it hadn't been for their sudden appearance, the two *Amis* fighters would have chopped them up into mincemeat, he was sure of that. The two pilots had obviously thought they were flying into a trap when they had spotted the deadly quadruple flak cannon that could fire a thousand 20mm shells a minute just beyond the ridge. At least, Scharf suspected that was what had happened.

For just as the wing man had come hurtling in at four hundred kilometres an hour ready for the kill, he had spotted the Italians, broken sharply to right in a manoeuvre which might well have torn the wing off his fighter, and had gone high into the sky, twisting and turning to avoid the flak shells which hadn't come. Seconds later, they had disappeared back the way they had come, and Scharf and the survivers of the feint attack had been saved.

Now as he slumped on the ground, all energy drained from his body, *Strega* bottle clutched to his chest, he said to an attentive Brandt, who hadn't been harmed in the attack, 'Casualties, Brandt?'

'Five dead, sir, and two wounded, not too badly, fortunately. The – er – girls are looking after their wounds.' He looked at the ground momentarily, as if to hide his embarrassment.

'Well, if those ladies-of-the-night are looking after 'em, Brandt, they're going to make a very rapid recovery – or snuff it *happily*.'

Now Brandt grinned too.

'All right, Brandt,' Scharf said, 'Let the men have their way with the whores; full precautions though. Parisians★ – the lot. I don't want my poor innocents coming down with what you would call a social disease.' He

★ *Army slang for a contraceptive.*

215

paused momentarily. 'And if you're inclined—'

'Oh no, sir, it wouldn't do as an officer. Not in front of the men,' Brandt interrupted hastily.

'Of course, of course,' Scharf agreed, tongue in cheek. 'Well, if you don't fancy the Italian ladies' ample charms ... and frankly, I must admit you're a bit of a fool for not doing so, young man. I mean, look at Adriana.'

Clambering on the flak cannon to hang out her dripping black bra, the Italian woman had somehow managed to get her left breast caught up in the camouflage webbing which covered it, and, swearing and panting, she was fighting hard to free herself.

'Well, try to find out what you can from that Macaroni officer. We might be able to use him.'

'Sir.' Brandt departed hastily, as if he were glad to do so, leaving a still-sitting Scharf to wonder about things, as he realized that those strange tracks he had discovered that night must have belonged to the looted Tommy trucks with their splendid real rubber tyres, which the girls used as their 'working area' when they had been employed servicing the Italian troops facing the Tommies.

For a few moments he forgot his planning. His men were preparing themselves for the whores. Some of them were even using the Italians' precious water to shave. He watched them like a proud father, happy for them. They deserved every little pleasure, however crude, that came their way. Their lives were, probably, short, savage and brutal. If they had to find their pleasure in this manner, so be it. What else remained for such men, 'hairy-assed stubble-hoppers', as they often called themselves? They were doomed as it was, and perhaps it was better that way. How could men who had been through the things they had in this war cope with post-war supposed civilization?

Then he dismissed the men; they lined up against the converted trucks where the little captain marched up and down, drinking *Strega* straight from the bottle and raising his feet high to crunch the imaginary rats that attempted to bar his progress.

Scharf had completed the mission that Field Marshal Rommel had given him. He had found a route through the 'Devil's Garden' which he felt would be suitable for the tanks and panzer grenadiers of the Tenth Panzer Division. He had discovered, too, that the *Ami* defences around the various passes, in particular at Faid, were poorly defended. With a bit of luck and with surprise on Rommel's side, the 'Desert Fox' should be able to break through with his lorried infantry. At the cost of a handful of his brave Brandenburgers, he had done what Rommel expected of him.

Suddenly, for some reason he couldn't explain at the time – it might have been exhaustion or just simply the *Strega* – he was sick of the war. He wanted to forget while he still had a chance, at least for a while.

Over at the cannon, the topless Adriana was still drying out her black bra, oblivious to the threats of the alcoholic officer who kept waving his overlong sword at her. Every now and again, as she occupied herself with her underwear, pressing and tugging at it, she threw come-hither looks over her shoulder at Scharf. He didn't need a crystal ball to know why. She wanted a bit from him. After all, he was an officer, and a German to boot. Probably she didn't service many of his rank and kind. Poor, stunted Sicilian peasant recruits would be her usual clients.

That didn't worry Scharf one little bit. Slowly, still clutching the bottle of *Strega* in his hand, he walked over to where she waited, her breasts uncovered, looking him firmly in the eye. '*Cara mia*,' she said, a little huskily, but not in the usual tone of a whore out for money in return for sex. 'You want fuck?' she added in German. She made her meaning quite clear by poking her finger through a circle made by the thumb and forefinger of her other hand.

'Yes, I like fuck,' he said baldly.

Her dark Italian eyes sparkled. She crooked a finger at him. 'Come ... here behind cannon.'

He needed no urging. He felt his loins thicken. She led him, swaying her broad hips provocatively, to the other side of the rusty flak gun, adorned by the whores' drying knickers.

There was a blanket there. She lay down on it without being asked. She raised her hips and, not taking her eyes off him for one moment, slipped off her knickers slowly. He didn't move immediately. She rubbed her pubic hairs, thick and coal black. The thin pink slit of her womanhood came into view. Now he felt himself really stiffen. She saw it. She opened her legs wider and flung out her arms to both sides, as if she were totally at his mercy and didn't give a damn about the fact.

He couldn't contain himself any longer. He let his ragged, smelly pants fall. Next moment he fell, too, right on to her soft, fleshy body. She gave a grunt. It was followed the next moment by another, this time of pleasure. Then the two of them were pounding away at each other, the others, the desert, the war totally forgotten, their only concern the mad, sweat-soaked world of their own pleasure...

'ROMMEL KOMMT ...
ROMMEL KOMMT.'

'With the Americans it is necessary to watch
your step and wrap anything one has to say
which is at the least critical or which savours
of advice in the most tactful language ...
They're a queer lot with many nice ones ...
So far as soldiering is concerned, believe me,
the British have nothing to learn from them.'
*British Corps Commander General
John Crocker to his wife, Jan 1943*

Hotel St Georges, Algiers, Feb 13th 1943

It was Saturday, but with things at the front the way they were, Eisenhower still came into his hotel headquarters to work. Often he felt there weren't enough hours in the day for all the tasks he had to complete. Nervously, he stubbed out the sixth Camel he had smoked since breakfast as he stepped out of his armoured Packard and took the salute of the sentries posted at the entrance to Supreme Headquarters.

Commander Butcher, formerly the vice-president of Columbia Broadcasting back in the States and now one of the new-fangled public relations men that all top US generals had added to their entourage of staff officers, welcomed him with a broad grin. 'Congratulations!' he cried happily.

Eisenhower, busy lighting yet another Camel of the sixty he'd probably smoke this Saturday, looked at Butcher's smiling face in bewilderment.

Butcher repeated the greeting and stretched out his hand.

Eisenhower didn't take it. 'What for?' he rasped. This Saturday he had no time for the usual foolishnesses of his 'gang', as he called his intimate circle of cronies and poker players.

'On becoming a full general. You've been awarded four stars by Congress, sir.'

'*What*?' Eisenhower exploded. He caught himself in time. An American general had always to pretend never to be interested in promotion. The standard formula at such times was always 'I was just doing my job'. 'How do you know?'

'Just had a phone call from Captain Fawkins of the submarine mother-ship *Maidstone* down in the harbour. He heard it on the BBC News. He wanted me to offer his congratulations.'

Eisenhower broke out in that famed ear-to-ear smile of his. Now he took the proferred hand. He had waited twenty-eight years for this moment. Now he had to hear the news indirectly through a foreign news service. It was surely a crazy world. 'I'm made a full general, Butch,' he said, a little peeved, pumping Butcher's hand up and down, 'and I'm not told of it. Well, maybe it isn't true. How did you hear of it, Butch?'

Butcher told him again. A moment later the phone rang urgently from the HQ's message centre. There the signallers had received an urgent teletype from Eisenhower's wife Mamie. For once, Mamie back in Washington was not nagging her husband, usually about suspected affairs with female members of his staff. Instead she had cabled, 'Congratulations on your fourth star.'

Finally Eisenhower believed the great news. All thoughts of the front and work this Saturday vanished. Immediately he called his staff together, including his 'darkies', as he called its black members, and promoted them one grade. Then he turned to a smiling Butcher as he dismissed the happy enlisted men, 'And you, Butch, can get your own aide.'

Like some dignitary of Ancient Rome, Eisenhower spread his largesse over everyone who worked for him directly or was close to him, save one person, though she meant more to him than all the others. In due course, later in the year, he would be prepared to give up a *fifth* star for the love of her. It was 'Civilian First Class' (as she called herself cynically), British driver-cum-secretary Kay Summersby.

But her turn would come soon enough. That afternoon, as the threat grew by leaps and bounds, the 'gang' celebrations went on and on. There was champagne, real French, plenty of it too. There was even Scotch, which was a rarity in Algiers.

Watching 'Ike', Kay Summersby told herself he was really enjoying himself, and he deserved it, for he hadn't had much fun in this life. She was right. Eisenhower's life as an adult had been the drudgery of remote garrison towns, the years of waiting for promotion, the picayune detail of peacetime soldiering in the United States, with not a war in sight; knowing that life was passing one by, drifting slowly into crotchety middle-age and retirement in Texas, where the living was cheap and the meagre Army pension might just be stretched from one retirement cheque to another.

But all that was forgotten now; Eisenhower had reached the top of his profession and he had a right to be a little drunk, which he was. When Butcher played his favourite record, *One Dozen Roses*, he insisted that his PR man should play it again and that they should all join in the chorus with him, as he sang the words in his unmusical voice, *'Gimme one dozen roses, put my heart beside them and send them to the girl I love.'* It was then that he looked longingly at the green-eyed former London model, and she knew which girl he'd like to send those 'dozen roses' to – and it wasn't Mamie in far-off Washington.

Thus they partied, sang and drank and enjoyed themselves with the gang, full of champagne and a little rationed Scotch, while five hundred miles away at the front, the storm was brewing, ready to break soon.

It was about eight, when Eisenhower's 'darkies' started to serve a special supper, including the smoked oysters which were the Supreme Commander's special favourite, that the first warning came in from General Anderson, the dour, awkward Scot in charge of the British First Army. He told a half-drunk Eisenhower that his army was on red alert. They had dug in in their hilltop positions, and were expecting a last, desperate German breakthrough attack.

Eisenhower didn't particularly like Anderson, and he knew the British Imperial General Staff didn't think much of the Scot either. So he wasn't particularly alarmed by the Britisher's dire warnings. He told Anderson to be on his guard and that he would reinforce the British First Army if the balloon really did go up. Then he put down his phone and, turning to Butcher, who was privy to most of his secrets, said, 'Anderson, a really nervous nelly, expecting the Krauts to attack.'

Butcher, flushed with drink, took his cue from Eisenhower, as he always did. 'Yes, a nervous nelly, sir. Don't think you'll have to grow my grey hairs worrying about him.'

Eisenhower laughed easily and smoothed his balding pate. 'Well, with the kind of hair

I have, Butch, I don't think I'll have to worry about hair, grey or otherwise.'

Butcher thrust a glass of Scotch at him. 'Last one of your ration, sir, I made it a big one. You'd better – er – enjoy it.' Over Eisenhower's shoulder, he winked knowingly at Kay Summersby, who was supping champagne delicately.

'Thanks, Butch.' For a minute, his good mood vanished and he seemed sober. 'I only hope that General Fredendall is on the ball this night. I'm afraid I picked a dud in Fredendall. All he goddam thinks about is building that damned underground HQ of his. I wish he'd concern himself about his front more.'

Butcher raised his own glass of Scotch in toast hastily. He didn't want anything to spoil the Supreme Commander's mood this special day. 'Here's to your health, sir ... and don't worry about General Fredendall. I'm sure he knows what he's doing. Now, what about going over to Kay and chatting to her, sir? You've neglected her. Take your mind off your problems.' He chanced a knowing wink.

'Get you,' Eisenhower agreed, the warning and the problem of Fredendall forgotten temporarily. 'Sure thing.' He nodded, and without making it too obvious, sidled over to where Kay stood – posed, would have been another word. 'God,' he said, breathing the odour of Scotch all over her, 'I'm a lucky old guy to have someone like you, Kay.'

'You're not old, General,' she replied in that charming soft Irish brogue of hers.

Eisenhower's heart leapt...

Outside it was dark now. Hundreds of miles away, the Second Corps front seemed calm. In their foxholes, the GIs twisted and turned under the cold spectral rays of the moon, trying to keep warm. For already, now the sun had gone down, it was going to be a night of bone-chilling cold. Soon it would be midnight and February 14th, 1943, St Valentine's Day, the day of young lovers. The Valentine that was soon to be presented to the thirty thousand green soldiers of Fredendall's Second Corps would not consist of one dozen roses, but it would be red all right – *blood red*.

But if the Second Corps front slept, Colonel Nichols and the 'Cherrypicker' at Fredendall's HQ didn't. Ever since they and the Jewish captain had squeezed the last bit of information they could out of the now very frightened Jenkins, who knew that his life was at stake, they had been trying to contact Eisenhower himself. Hurwitz, the American captain, had been aghast at the suggestion that such lowly officers as they should approach Supreme Headquarters without going through 'channels', which meant Fredendall. But the 'Cherrypicker' had soon set him to rights with, 'Captain, even generals wet their knickers at times. Let's have a go.' To which Nichols had chortled in admiration, 'well said, Sergeant, the true voice of the people. The voice of the common man, the voice of the future.'

The 'Cherrypicker' had flushed with embarrassment. He knew the Colonel was very smart, but naturally totally barmy.

But the voice of the common man's suggestion, as well intended as it was, didn't work at Supreme Headquarters. The top brass, celebrating Eisenhower's fourth star, weren't listening. Time and time again, they tried, hunched in the overheated radio shack, their faces as if glazed with Vaseline in the glaring white light of the hissing Coleman lamp. Without success.

Even when Nichols used all the authority which Eisenhower had personally given him, he didn't manage to get through. As some snotty staff officer said, 'Listen Colonel, if you told me that Rommel personally was standing outside this goddam door, armed with a .45 just about to assassinate Ike, I wouldn't dare to disturb him just now. Blast and damn, can't you understand that the Supreme Commander is celebrating an important promotion? If I disturbed him, I'd be demoted to the lowest form of enlisted man cleaning out crappers in Alaska or somewhere. Try tomorrow once the chief's recovered from his hangover. Over and out.' And with that, he slammed down the phone and Nichols knew he had lost.

'Sorry,' the little American captain said, seeing the crestfallen look on the Britisher's face. 'But you've got to understand, Colonel, that's the way the Regular Army works. They can always have a war, but promotion is something different...' He paused when Nichols didn't respond, before asking, 'What now, Colonel?'

Nichols pulled himself together and wondered how his fellow dons, who taught history back at Oxford, would have treated something like this. He'd hear them go on about Napoleon and his gippy tummy at the Battle of Waterloo and the like. But what would they make of a commander who was preoccupied with promotion on the eve of a great battle? But then, he concluded, they'd probably never heard of Eisenhower and his fourth star. 'What now?' he echoed. 'I'll tell you, Hurwitz. I am going to test my theory. I'm going to take the jeep – you too –' he looked at the 'Cherrypicker' – 'and we're going to see if the Germans really attack where I think they will.'

'The Faid Pass, Colonel?'

'No. Kasserine.'

'*Kasserine*, sir? But—'

Nichols didn't give the American Intelligence officer a chance to finish. Instead he interrupted with, 'I know I'm going to trot out a tired old cliché. But in war, my dear Hurwitz, always expect the unexpected...'

En Route for the Kasserine Pass, the Night of 13th/14th Feb 1943.

Despite his apparent levity, Nichols's pride had been hurt. As they rolled through the silver desert, starkly outlined by the cold light of an unfeeling moon, huddled in greatcoats and whatever else they could find to keep out the biting night air, he considered his position this Saturday to Sunday night.

He had been in Intelligence ever since he had volunteered for the Intelligence Corps in September 1939 – and he had been damned good in his own particular field, too. He knew that. With his unsoldierly ways and rather donnish manner, he would never otherwise have achieved the rank of Colonel at his young age and with his unorthodox approach, especially in the Western Desert, when intelligence officers had come and gone with each new failure.

Montgomery had recommended him personally to Supreme Headquarters. There,

Eisenhower had sent him as a kind of un-official Supreme Commander's representative to Fredendall's Corps. There, he had virtually spied on the Americans on Eisenhower's behalf. It had not been a task to his liking: an Englishman spying on Yanks for another Yank. But he had carried out the task faithfully and objectively enough despite the definitely anti-British attitude of the Yanks, from Fredendall right on down to the simplest private first class.

Now when the balloon was about to go up (Jenkins's confession about the Brandenburgers had made that quite clear), no one was listening to him. A potential tragedy was on the way, which might affect not only the US Army in Tunisia, but the British; and the British had suffered far too many hard knocks in North Africa since 1940 to be cheated out of their victory now. Besides, the long-suffering, half-starved British people back home needed a victory. All they had known since the outbreak of war was defeat after defeat – Norway, France, Greece, Africa ... it had been endless.

Nichols pulled a face as they bumped and rumbled in the jeep across the endless plain. To his right, where the Faid Plain was located, he thought he could see light: the silent pink wavering and flashing of an artillery duel. But when the light vanished after a few minutes, he told himself he had to be seeing things. Perhaps it was wishful thinking; he wanted confirmation of his worst fears.

He tried to force his mind on to other matters, burying his head deeper into the collar of his greatcoat which, like all the greatcoats he had ever worn, smelled of horses and horse manure. For a moment or two he wondered why, in his donnish manner, trying to work out the details. In the end, he gave in and resorted to the old trick of breathing out hard so that his warm breath swept up the collar and partially warmed his red, freezingly cold ears.

Suddenly, for no particular reason, he remembered the end of his first and most expensive greatcoat. It had been during the retreat to Dunkirk in May 1940. He had been the youngest subaltern in his unit, which was made up of regulars and World War One reservists, hearty, red-faced officers with a chestful of medal ribbons and nicknames such as 'Jumbo', 'Blackie' and 'Hairless Harry', which indicated their physical appearance and past places of service all over the Empire. He had been the only one without a nickname, save for an occasional 'Prof', and he was the one who had always been given the most unpleasant tasks.

That May day with the Germans at their

heels, he had been appointed by the rest, who didn't seem one bit bothered that the 'Hun' might arrive at any moment, to stand look-out in the upper room of some vanished coal-miner's cottage near Bethune. The others, for their part, had busily looted the house for what they could find to eat and drink – mostly drink. So, while down below they swallowed the rough, working-class *'pinot'* straight from the bottle, laughing and joking as if they were back home at some boozy mess party, he watched the cobbled straight road that led from the nearest town, his stomach rumbling crazily, watching for the first appearance of the 'Hun', as the old sweats called the triumphant Germans.

What had happened then, had happened so quickly and violently that years later he had difficulty in remembering the course of events, save that they had ruined his best greatcoat, bought at great expense (to his now-dead father) after he had been commissioned and had given him his unlikely name of 'Crasher'.

The German tank had turned the corner and had belched fire immediately.

The shell had hit the roof, the upper floor had collapsed, and he had fallen through it in a cloud of dust and broken lathes, crashing right through into the muck-filled pig sty attached to the miner's cottage, where 'Bimbasher' Hargreaves, once of the Sudan Defence Front, was crouched among the alarmed pigs, trying to evacuate his reluctant bowels.

The old sweats had hooted with laughter at the sight of him, accompanied by an indignant 'Bimbasher' Hargreaves, braces dangling, hand clutching a wad of 'Army Form Blank'*, who was crying, 'Bloody fellah came crashing in on me while I was clearing my bowels ... Is there no peace for a chap in this ruddy war ... crashed right in on me...'

While he had tugged off the messy greatcoat to cries of 'What a pong!' on the part of his fellow officers, one of them, 'Bunny' O'Hare, if he remembered correctly, had chortled, totally ignoring the bullets spraying the front of the cottage, 'Chap needs a new name, fellahs ... What about "Crasher?"' So, at the cost of one expensive greatcoat and a shock to the nerves, young Second Lieutenant Nichols, owlish, bespectacled and in no way soldierly, had become 'Crasher'.

He smiled fondly at the memory of what now seemed another age. But not for long. At the wheel, the 'Cherrypicker' burst into his reverie with an urgent, tense, 'Sir, three o'clock – trouble!'

*Official British Army designation for lavatory paper.

'Crasher' Nicols swung his head to the right where the Faid Pass lay. The American Intelligence officer did the same, face a little puzzled by what he saw there.

Once more there was that silent, flickering pink light over the pass held by Fredendall's Second Corps. But this time, there were also red flares sailing into the night sky to hang there for what seemed an age, before dropping to the earth like fallen angels.

'Signal flares,' Nichols said before he was asked. 'Signal flares, summoning help. Your people are in trouble.'

'Over there, too, sir,' the 'Cherrypicker' butted in. 'At one o'clock.'

By now, the American had understood the British Army's way of pointing out direction, based on the clock face. Automatically, he turned to the left with Nichols. Faintly, but definitely there, the three of them could see the high-speed Morse-like zip-zap of tracer speeding to and fro silently.

Nichols felt a sense of triumph, but he didn't express it aloud, especially to the young American Hurwitz, whom he had grown to like. 'The Kasserine Pass,' he said. 'There's a fire fight going on up there. The Jerries are attacking.'

'Then you were right, sir,' Hurwitz exclaimed excitedly. 'The Faid's a feint. The real Jerry objective is the Kass—'

'Let's go and look-see, Hurwitz,' Nichols cut him off sharply. He didn't want the American to be forced to eat humble pie. He didn't deserve to have to.

The 'Cherrypicker' put his foot down hard. They swept on, watched now by the little group of men waiting in the defile in front of them, with a tall, lean *Wehrmacht* officer following the jeep's progress through his night glasses.

Under normal circumstances, Scharf and his Brandenburgers wouldn't have concerned themselves with one single jeep. Not now, however. For behind the little advance group were lined up all Rommel's precious Tiger tanks. In darkness, without infantry protection, the sixty-ton metal monsters were very vulnerable. A daring *Ami* armed with one of their new bazookas could easily sneak up on a tank and at close range blow the hell out of it. On such occasions, any lucky 'David' could put a swift end to the giant 'Goliath's' life. Hence Scharf waited, while behind him, Hartmann placed the 'oven pipe', as the old hares called their own rocket launcher, to his brawny shoulder, and prepared to fire.

Scharf tensed. The jeep had come to a little crossroads. It was the moment of truth, Scharf told himself, though the enemy didn't know that. If the jeep turned left, he'd let it go on its way unharmed. If it turned right towards the gully where the Tigers waited for their order to attack, he'd command Hartmann to fire – and that would be that. For a brief second, he thought how easily human life could be extinguished. It hung on a whim, a wrong turn, a frail thread that made the difference between life and death.

At the little crossroads, the 'Cherrypicker' hesitated. An old desert hand, who knew if you made a wrong turn 'up the blue'*, you might end up dead from thirst or starvation or because your petrol ran out, the NCO was cautious by nature. Then he made his decision, as he heard the first boom of heavy artillery coming faintly from the Kasserine Pass. He turned right.

Crouched there in the cold silver darkness, Scharf let his night glasses drop swiftly. 'Hartmann,' he commanded.

'Ready, sir,' the ex-legionnaire snapped back. As always, he was ready for death. It seemed to Scharf he was one of the few soldiers he had ever encountered who actually enjoyed killing people in battle.

Scharf counted off the metres silently. He could afford to let Hartmann do it, with the clumsy weapon he now balanced on his big shoulder, eye glued to the sight. Now he could see the outlines of three men, slumped

* Eighth Army slang for the desert frontline.

239

as if they were very tired, in the jeep's seats. Cynically he told himself, and regretted the thought the very next moment, that they'd be sleeping for good in a few seconds.

'Take aim, Hartmann, now,' he hissed.

The big sergeant had already done so.

Scharf counted off the last three seconds. '*One ... two...*' The jeep was so close now that even the worst shot among his German-Americans couldn't miss. '*Three.*' He hesitated no longer. '*FIRE!*'

Hartmann's finger curled round the trigger of the clumsy-looking weapon. He jerked it back. An explosion. The tube jumped on his shoulder. A blast of hot, acrid air. A streak of angry red flame shot from the weapon's back, and then the black blob of the armour-piercing rocket-bomb was hurrying towards the unsuspecting jeep. A clash of metal on metal. The jeep reared up on its back wheels. Tyres exploded. A blinding flash. The bonnet flew open. A shriek of absolute agony, and the jeep collapsed, a smoking broken wreck, with someone moaning, 'Oh my leg ... God Almighty, my leg...'

Cautiously, Scharf moved forward to the spot from where that awful screaming came. In his right hand, he clutched his pistol. Despite the freezing cold, his hand was wet with sweat. He knew why. It wasn't fear; it was tension. For he knew what he must do.

He had to put the man crying in pain out of his misery. It would be an act of mercy, but also one of self-protection. He did not want anyone else to be alerted by that terrible wail of agony.

He paused at the driver. He was dead behind the wheel. The steering column had pierced his heart like a spear. He had been killed instantly. Behind him there was a small, dark officer, wracked with pain. The years of Nazi Aryan doctrine told him that the American was a Jew. How many times had he been through the boring theory of how to recognize 'the Eternal Jewish Parasite', as the Nazi lecturers always called the 'racial enemy'. This particular 'racial enemy', however, was still alive, though obviously very badly wounded. For one long moment, Scharf considered shooting him on the spot. If the wounded American Jew fell into the clutches of some Nazi thug, he'd be shot out of hand.

'*Mom*,' the wounded man moaned. 'Please Mom, I'm hurt.'

Scharf recognized the plea, all right. He changed his mind at once. He fumbled inside the jeep until he found what he wanted. The enemy always carried little syringes – simple devices, filled with morphia. Hastily he pulled up the man's right sleeve, pressed the needle against his upper arm, and injected the pain-killing drug. Then, as an after-thought, he opened the officer's collar, pulled off the metal dog tag, and threw it as far away as he could. He knew the enemy marked their dog tags with the owner's religion, and this particular *Ami*'s tag would signify death if the man fell into the hands of some fanatic Jew-hater.

Finally he turned to Nichols. The latter was obviously badly hurt. In the cold silver light of the moon, Scharf could see just how pale the enemy was. His nostrils were pinched, too – another bad sign. But the English colonel was still conscious, and Scharf had the feeling he would survive.

'*Es ist mein Bein,*' he was surprised to hear the officer say in excellent, almost accent-free German. '*Wie sieht es aus?*'

In reality, he had no time to see how the Englishman's leg looked. But that German did it. The enemy officer had to be a cultured person, who had obviously studied German in Germany at one time or other. '*Ein Moment,*' Scarf answered. '*Ich werde mir das ansehen.*'

He gasped when he saw the Englishman's leg in the moonlight. It was a mess. He told himself that any German field surgeon would have amputated it at once. Still, Scharf reminded himself, there probably wasn't a surgeon within fifty square kilometres of where they were now. The English-man would be lucky if he were picked up by frontline stretcher-bearers and taken to the nearest field dressing station, where he might be patched up in time. If he weren't – Scharf didn't think that particularly unpleasant thought to an end. Instead, he asked urgently, knowing that time was slipping away rapidly and he had no business wasting it on the enemy soldier who could well die before the day was out, 'Where's your field dressing?'

'In the camouflage netting of my helmet,' Nichols answered weakly. He felt his strength ebbing now, but he fought to retain consciousness. It was better for his chances of survival that way.

Hastily Scharf pulled the big wadded yellow pad from beneath Nichols's helmet. He opened it, knowing that his hands were filthy, but that he couldn't worry about hospital-type sterility now. As gently as he could, he placed the pad over the gaping wound just behind the knee. Fortunately, the shock of the shell's impact had reduced the amount of bleeding, so he could see what he was doing. 'This is going to hurt,' he muttered through gritted teeth.

Behind him, someone was saying some way off, *Rommel ... Rommel kommt...*' He ignored the news and concentrated on tying the bandage as tightly as possible, while Nichols moaned softly. 'Loosen it at intervals,' he commanded. 'I don't want to cut off the blood supply too much.'

Nichols nooded his head feebly. In a minute he knew he'd faint.

'*Rommel kommt ... Rommel*—'

'Keep in the open ... near the jeep,' Scharf said, wiping his bloody hands on the ground and then on Nichols's tunic. 'The stretcher-bearers'll see you better.' Without turning round to an excited Hartmann, who was looting the wrecked jeep, oblivious to the fact that the 'Desert Fox' himself was on his way, he ordered, 'Upturn that rifle as a marker, Hartmann.'

'Sir.'

Dutifully, crunching a blood-soaked American Hershey bar, Hartmann did as he was told. He thrust the M-1 rifle, muzzle downwards, into the earth. It was the traditional marker for medics looking for casualties on the battlefield.

Scharf patted Nichols and lied, 'You'll be all right now, Colonel. Just stay in sight. If you hear any German spoken, shout up. It could be our medics.'

'I will...' Nichols fought off the dark veil of unconsciousness which threatened to submerge him and added, 'Thank you ... You have been ... a gentleman.'

Scharf laughed a little cynically. 'I'm afraid the days of gentlemen on the battlefield are over, *Herr Oberst*.' He straightened up. The warning, '*Rommel kommt*,' was getting louder and louder. Behind him in the wadi, he could hear the tank commanders giving out their orders to the crews of the Tigers. Scharf touched his hand briefly to his peaked cap in salute.

On the ground, Nichols tried to do the same, but failed miserably; he simply didn't have the strength. A little voice at the back of his brain sneered, 'God, you can't even play the gallant soldier on the field of battle, your last battle. Nichols, you'll never make a proper soldier if you live to be a hundred, something which I doubt you will.'

Then Major Scharf was striding back to his vehicle. Everywhere there was the sudden roar of trucks and tanks being started. Nichols winced as red-hot pain stabbed up through his wounded leg like a burning poker. The German had been very fair, but frontline soldiers usually were. It was the swine at the rear who were the bastards. Still, he didn't want to fall into German hands either at the front or to the rear. With the last of his strength, feeling the blood soaking through the bandage, he rolled to the side of the track into the dark shadow cast by a bunch of camel thorn. Perhaps he could hide there till dawn, when the Yanks might find him. Anything was better than spending the rest of the war behind barbed wire in the POW cage. He groaned again, and knew he was losing consciousness at last. He did slowly, with that cry the final thing he heard that St Valentine's Day, 1943. *'Rommel kommt ... Rommel kommt...'*

THE BATTLE OF THE KASSERINE PASS

'It takes 16,000 dead to train a major-general'

French Marshal Joffree, 1916

Battlefront, Second US Corps, Feb 14th 1943

Eagerly the triumphant young panzer grenadiers of the Tenth Panzer Division were slipping into their combat packs on all sides. Those armed with fearsome flame throwers were lining themselves up with their bodyguard riflemen. Hoarse, red-faced NCOs were handing out extra stick grenades. The young soldiers, sensing victory over the *Amis*, were grabbing them like ice-cream cones and thrusting them down the sides of their jackboots. Behind them, the black-uniformed tank crews were clambering up the steel hides of their tanks. Easily, they swung themselves into the tight turrets and settled behind their cannons and instruments. Hastily, the mechanics handed up more shells for the racks on both sides of the cupolas. Everything was controlled chaos. Time was of the essence. For it was clear they had caught the *Amis* by complete surprise. They were pulling back everywhere, and even the most stupid of the attackers knew they had to keep up the pressure relentlessly now.

When here and there a more nervous trooper stopped to urinate, some hard-faced NCO would guffaw, 'What d'yer think this is, arse-with-ears, the sodding piss-corner in the local inn. This is a battlefield, sonny. Stuff that ugly thing away – *at once!*' And they did.

Now, on all sides, as the tankers chewed their special combat chocolate, filled with vitamins, the companies reported in: 'First Company ready, sir ... Second Company ready, sir...' On and on along the line of steel monsters, as above their heads the shells hissed and whined towards the crumbling enemy positions with banshee-like howls, and further back the heavies opened up, as if the door of some gigantic blast furnace had just been flung to one side.

Then they were moving. Slowly at first. But the rusty metallic clanking soon turned to a high-pitched roar. They started to race across the plain, throwing up great wakes of sand behind them. The frightened, almost panicked *Ami* gunners took up the challenge for a few minutes. Cherry-red flame slashed the morning haze. White tracer shot across the intervening space as the tanks came closer and closer. Here and there, the US gunners struck lucky as a German tank rumbled to a slow stop, a burst track unfolding behind it like a broken limb. But not many. The American anti-tank shells simply couldn't penetrate the German tanks' thick steel hide. They bounced off uselessly, like glowing golf balls. On and on the tanks came, now in a great extended V with the horns beginning to curl inwards. The gunners knew what that meant. The Krauts were attempting to outflank them, cut them off, trap them, mow them down mercilessly from behind.

They started to break. In ones and twos at first, slipping from behind the shields of their puny 57mm cannon and making a run for it, with machine gunfire stitching a pattern of death at their flying feet. Then in groups – a dozen, a score, half a hundred – making no attempt to appear as if they were pulling back under orders. Here and there, officers, sweating and frantic, drawn 45 Colts in their hands tried to stop them, like children playing a game of tag in a schoolyard. In vain. There was no stopping the fleeing men.

Behind them, the Shermans of the first US Armoured Division, preparing for a counterattack, were seized by the panic, too. As the first of the thirty-ton tanks began to blaze furiously, other crews whose vehicles had not yet been hit flung themselves out of the US tanks, pulling off their radio leads and even the leather helmets they wore, and started to pelt to the rear. The rot was setting in on all sides – and now the advancing Germans were singing as they rolled forward, crushing guns and gunners beneath their blood-red tracks. Victory was in the very air and they were no longer afraid. The *Amis* were on the run...

At Fredendall's headquarters, all was latent panic and open confusion. Telephones jangled. Teleprinters clattered. Motorcycle dispatch riders roared back and forth, carrying urgent messages to and from the front. Staff officers stumbled and ran down the dim, half-finished underground corridors, trying to find someone to report to or pass on their message of doom and gloom. Senior officers whispered instructions to their 'strikers'*, telling them what to pack *now* – just in case. Others poured over maps, filling ever more rapidly with red chinograph markings indicating yet further enemy advances.

Here and there, some few officers of Fredendall's green staff kept their heads.

When the Germans closed in, gunners manning the howitzers so that they were firing over the heads of the advancing enemy, they knew what to do. They ordered the powder charges, used to fire the howitzer

*US Army usage for 'batmen'.

shells, to be reduced from strength six to strength four, so that the missiles wouldn't carry so far. Infantry, about ready to break and flee, according to their commanders, were reassured that massed US and Allied fighters were on their way to give them cover. They were to stay in their posts. It was a lie, but the staff officers knew it would keep the 'doughs' from running for the time being. But the first planes that would appear that terrible dawn would be those of the enemy. Antiquated Stukas, which flung themselves from the grey sky as if they were about to smash themselves on the ground, their sirens shrieking, a myriad of steel eggs tumbling lethally from their blue-painted bellies.

'Everything's against us,' Fredendall moaned, head in hands, when he heard of the Stuka attack. 'Even the flyboys are letting Second Corps down.'

Fredendall had every reason to feel depressed. Not that the supreme egoist would ever admit it, but he had failed to organize his corps ready for a German attack, although he had ample warnings. In one armoured formation alone, commanded by the old tippler who had kissed Kay Summersby's hand during Eisenhower's visit to the front, two battalions were surrounded and three were on the way to obliteration.

Eisenhower had rushed to the front that early Sunday morning. He had been depressed by what he had seen, but he didn't criticize Fredendall, though later, when the full extent of defeat became clear, he realized he should have done. Instead, he signalled the US chiefs-of-staff in Washington: 'I really believe that fighting today will show that our troops are giving a very fine account of themselves, even though we must give up part of our extended line.'

The truth was harsh. The French troops, who had helped the Americans to defend the Faid Pass, fled, abandoning their hospital, giving away everything they couldn't take with them. But the rear echelon GIs didn't wait to be given, they looted. As hundreds of hollow-eyed infantry from the shattered frontline American battalions flooded the rear, the GIs took off with alarm clocks, bottles of peach brandy, even letter openers. In the nearby US field hospital, packed with six hundred wounded and badly burnt American casualties, the harassed medical orderlies gave pint after pint of their own blood for transfusions until the order came (from whom, no one ever knew): 'pack and run!'

The medics did that, swaddling the worst casualties in blankets and hoisting them into open trucks, which would drive without lights for fear of being spotted by the Germans. 'Retreat,' one of the supervising surgeons commented. A sardonic, lightly wounded GI, trying to write home, scribbled on the air mail letter form, 'Americans never retreat, they *withdraw*.'

Now Fredendall was finally realizing the vulnerability of the Kasserine Pass position. In that general area, the Second Corps men had already suffered appalling losses. Fredendall's 168th Infantry Regiment, which had started out that fatal Valentine's Day with 189 officers and 3,728 enlisted men, was now down to 50 officers and 1,000 soldiers. Another regiment had lost three colonels, fifty-two other officers and 1,526 men.

Fredendall sent out his air reconnaissance and artillery spotter planes to find out the extent of the tragedy. All that night, they would swoop out low over the German positions, dropping blood-red flares to illuminate the scene below. It was frightening. In the immediate area, the pilots spotted forty-four tanks, fifty-nine halftracks, twenty-two trucks and twenty-six artillery pieces, all abandoned by their panicked crews, some of the equipment still burning.

Now, at last, Fredendall acted. He ordered more troops up to the Kasserine Pass in order to bring up the number of defenders to two thousand men. That night, Fredendall called Colonel Alex Stark, commanding the Twenty-Sixth Infantry Regiment, and told him, 'Alex, I want you to go to Kasserine right away and pull a Stonewall Jackson. Take over up there.'

Stark hesitated. 'You mean tonight, General?'

'Yes, right away.'

Stark knew the difficulties facing him that night of terrible confusion, but he knew Fredendall's hair-trigger temper too. He didn't argue. For the next twelve hours, he drove through the night, full of artillery fire and the thud of bombs, being stopped all the time by nervous sentries with the challenge 'Snafu', to which he had to reply wearily, 'Damned right.' Later it seemed the challenge and countersign fitted the confused situation perfectly, but that was later. When he arrived at the fatal pass at seven the next morning, even Stonewall Jackson, that hero of the Civil War, would have given up when he'd seen what was available to Colonel Stark.

There was only one troop of infantry in a proper defensive position. Both sides of the pass were defended by four companies of infantry, which couldn't give each other mutual support. The thousands of mines supposedly in position to stop enemy tanks and infantry had simply been dumped on the tracks and not buried, and the Germans were attacking through the surrounding hills, attempting to turn the flanks of this latter-day Stonewall Jackson.

About that time, a British brigadier from Montgomery's Twenty-Sixth Armoured Brigade came up to help. Stark told him he had the situation 'well in hand'. The brigadier thought he hadn't. He went forward to see for himself. Moments later, he came flying back in his staff car, followed by a hail of German fire. He reported back to his superiors, Stark 'had completely lost control of the situation ... I thought Stark a nice boy – gallant but quite out his depth.' As for Stark, he dubbed the British intruder 'a blockhead'. Even with disaster looming at any moment, the two 'cousins from across the sea', as the British Premier Churchill dubbed his American allies, could not forbear their squabbling...

The Oasis at Kasserine, Feb 16th 1943

For a while, the front had been silent. The German attackers had seemingly broken off their attack on the Kasserine Pass. Here and there, small US patrols were venturing out to check what had happened. Down below, the box-like Red Cross ambulances were scurry-

257

ing back and forth, collecting the groaning, moaning wounded. A few of the GI defenders were bold enough to attempt to heat themselves up a cup of coffee using camel thorn or the waxed containers of the K rations. One or two of the infantry even tried to loot the dead.

Not for long. On the stroke of ten, there was a tremendous, earth-shaking roar, which drowned out the noise of the tanks starting up for the last attack. With a hoarse, exultant scream, the whole weight of a German divisional artillery sped over the hills and slammed into the American positions. The shells burst with a mighty crash. Whole lengths of the US line vanished. Everywhere dugouts crumbled, burying the defenders alive. Ambulances flew into the air, throwing out their wounded. Fresh Shermans coming up to support Stark were swiped off the plain, as if they were insignificant beetles struck by a giant's hand.

And still the German guns rumbled and thundered. The first red-hot sighing became a scream, a monstrous, baleful scream. It rose and rose in fury, elemental, but man-made and controlled. The defenders shrieked silently, crazed at that terrible noise. Others flung their hands to their ears, trying to blot it out like frightened children trying to eradicate a nightmare. Men went mad.

Others flung away their weapons, scrambled from the holes and ran blindly through the shell bursts like professional footballers, zigzagging to left and right until, finally, inevitably, the shells caught up with them and they disintegrated in balls of furious red and yellow explosive.

The heavy artillery moved on to the rear American positions. The cannons were replaced by the six-barrelled multiple mortars, the 'screaming meemies'. From their position closer to where the surviving Americans were, the gunners pressed the buttons which activated the mortars' electric firing mechanism. There was a sound like someone hitting the bass notes on some monstrous piano. It was followed by a grating noise. It was as if a diamond was being run across glass. Abruptly, the air above the Americans was filled with heavy canopies of bombs. With a series of tremendous crashes, they fell out of the sky and slammed into the defensive works. Salvo after frightening salvo. Red-hot shards of jagged metal flew on all sides. Men were beheaded. Others had their limbs torn off. Men were cut into jagged pieces like the work of some butcher's apprentice gone mad and clumsy. Red, gory, steaming offal piled up, as if outside an abbatoir working full out.

'Roll 'em!' the German tank commanders

ordered.

Behind the Mark IV's, the infantry crouched tightly in their 'grapes', using the tanks' steel hides as protection.

'Number One company ... two company ... three company'; the orders came thick and fast. '... *ROLL!*'

Watching the Tigers, the centre of the striking force, ready to go on, watched further back by Rommel himself, Scharf told himself he had done all he could do. Next to him, Lieutenant Brandt, his face glowing with youthful enthusiasm, yelled above that tremendous, ear-splitting racket, 'What a spectacle, sir! Only we Germans could do this!'

Scharf nodded, but didn't comment.

'Fire smoke,' the commandant of the leading Tiger bellowed. 'Roll 'em!'

With a great lurch, the sixty-ton monster moved from its 'hide', the smoke dischargers on both sides of the turret firing smoke bombs to left and right. They burst at once. Thick white smoke billowed up in a cloud. Rusty springs creaking, its long overhanging gun moving from left to right like the snout of some monster seeking out its prey, the first Tiger swept ponderously into the final battle. One by one, the rest of the Tiger company followed, its crews knowing that nothing the *Amis* had could stop them now. They were invincible, the most powerful tanks in the whole world.

Scharf touched his hand to his battered peaked cap in a kind of a salute.

Brandt looked at him in wonder.

Scharf thought the one-armed lieutenant deserved an explanation. 'It's the last time, Brandt. The last victory. We'll never see this again in Africa, I'm afraid.' He paused as yet another Tiger rumbled by, drowning out the sound of battle with the roar of its 400 HP engine.

'But if we can build tanks like that, sir,' Brandt shouted as it passed in a cloud of dust and sand, 'what can stop Germany? We might not have all the men, but those Tiger—'

'It's a pious hope, my dear Lieutenant. Still, we're not supposed to worry about such important things.' He gave a weary grin. 'We're plain, old, broken-down stubble-hoppers. It's our fate in life to fight and die and – hopefully – make a handsome corpse.' He rose from his squatting position. 'Come on, Brandt, let's see what those damned looters of ours, masquerading as soldiers, are up to...'

But the 'damned looters masquerading as soldiers' were no longer looting. Even the most hard-boiled among them, such as Sergeant Hartmann, wouldn't have dared to do that at this moment. Instead, they were either standing stiffly to attention, with their right arms extended in the 'German greeting',* or they were cheering wildly as the cavalcade drew ever closer. A minute later, when Scharf and Brandt saw the reason for the reassertion of military discipline among their ragged, battle-worn Brandenburgers, they did the same. For the 'Desert Fox' himself was now entering the battered oasis, where dead Americans sprawled on both sides of the track in the dramatic poses of those done violently to death. And Scharf, who had known Rommel for so long, could see that the 'Desert Fox' was enjoying every minute of his triumph, even the cheers of the Arabs, who had been looting the American stores a few seconds before.

The old feelings were stirring, it was clear, in the Field Marshal's sick body. For him, it must have been like the great days when Montgomery's Tommies had been fleeing towards Egypt, leaving the roads behind them choked with booty. Now it was the turn of the Americans to flee, and the Arabs were cheering again. *'Hitler ... Hitler,'* the ragged throng called over and over again. And then *'Rommel ... Rommel ... ROMMEL!'* Happily, the 'Desert Fox' waved his fly whisk

Name for the 'Heil Hitler' salute.

in response, perhaps forgetting that in a day or so the same Arabs might well be looting his supply lines and stores. But that didn't matter at this moment of triumph.

The little cavalcade rolled to a stop inside the oasis. Rommel's big car was surrounded by a throng of cheering Arabs. All around them lay dead Americans and Arabs. The night before, the panicked American supply troops had blown up the Kasserine ammunition dump. They had been indifferent to the fate of the locals. Nearly a hundred men, women and children had gone up in the explosion. But then, Scharf told himself, the Arabs thought life cheap.

Suddenly Rommel caught sight of the two Brandenburg officers. He cried something to his adjutant and yelled to Scharf, 'Over here, Scharf.' As the young officer pulled out his pistol and threatened the Arabs so that they moved back a few paces, still cheering wildly and crying *'Rommel ... Rommel'*, Scharf and Brandt hurried over. Clicking to attention, Scharf started to report in the traditional *Wehrmacht* fashion. Rommel waved his fly whisk for him to desist. 'Well, Scharf,' he said in a somewhat tired voice, 'We did it again, eh ... In a way, thanks to you and your fellows. We took the *Amis* by surprise, didn't we?'

'Yessir,' Scharf replied dutifully, though he

was pleased that the Field Marshal had spotted and congratulated him at this moment of his first victory over the Americans.

Rommel looked thoughtful, and his joyful appearance gave way to that of the sick man Scharf had only known for these last months in North Africa.

'I had not intended a major push,' he mused, almost as if he were talking to himself. 'Now I don't know. The Americans have been easy meat. They are still green, unlike that devil Montgomery's fellows.' He licked his cracked lips, surrounded by desert sores. 'Perhaps I could exploit this local victory.'

Scharf felt it was his duty to ask how, for it seemed that the 'Desert Fox' expected him to.

'How?' Rommel repeated thoughtfully. 'Together with General von Arnim's Fifth I could push through Kasserine, and in a double-pronged assault, make a major victory of this little one. The Americans will take a long time to recover. Green troops usually do. Montgomery will have to stay behind his defences at Mareth till the mess down here is sorted out, and then it will be spring.' He shrugged his now skinny shoulders, and his heavy leather coat creaked as he did so. 'And in spring, as we all know, my dear Scharf, a *new* spring, lots of changes ... Lots of things can happen...'

But even as he said the words, his voice seemed to fade, and suddenly Scharf realized that Rommel really didn't believe his own words. There'd be no new spring for the 'Desert Fox' and his *Afrikakorps*. Rommel had achieved his last victory in Africa...

Two weeks later it was all over. British Field Marshal Alexander, known universally, even by his own wife, as 'Alex', who once had commanded German troops himself, took command. He was completely disgusted with the Americans under his command. He thought them utterly green and not yet ready for battle. With Fredendall 'kicked upstairs' and sent back to the States as a lieutenant general to some sort of training command, 'Alex' could impose his will, not only on his British troops, but on those of the battered US Second Corps, which had suffered six thousand casualties. Two weeks after the defeat at Kasserine, he issued a confident order of the day to the 'Soldiers of the Allies'. It stated: 'The enemy is making a desperate bid to break through ... Stand firm. Fight and kill the enemy. A great Allied victory is within grasp if every soldier does his duty.'

But the Germans didn't come again that day. For the night before, under the cover of darkness, they had commenced their retreat.

The Germans were fleeing like the *Amis* had done. Behind them, in their panic, they left their equipment and their booty. Kasserine again became American, and in years to come, Eisenhower would always remember that 'damned place in Africa' where he had suffered his first defeat at the same time that he had been awarded his fourth star.

That day Rommel came up to the front for the last time. It was as if he intended to savour the awesome, terrible majesty of the battlefield just once more. But it was too much for him. For the guns on both sides were keeping up a constant, frenzied tattoo of shelling. It was as bad as he had experienced in the trenches of the 'Old War' as a young officer. It was decided to retire to the safety of his armoured truck. For once, he was not prepared to risk his life with his forward troops, as he had done so often before. Instead, he slumped in the leather seat, his face as sombre as his thoughts.

Like a twentieth-century Hannibal, he had fought his last battle in Africa, close to where that celebrated warrior had fought his at Zama, a score of kilometres from Kasserine. Soon he'd be on his way home. In just a year and a bit from now, he'd be dead, killed not by the enemy, but his own hand: forced to take poison in retaliation for the support he had given to the plotters against Hitler.

Curiously enough, as the armoured truck bogged down in the Tunisian mud, the officer who would trigger off that chain of events which would result in Rommel's death took charge of getting the heavy vehicle and its illustrious occupant on its way again. He was Colonel Klaus von Stauffenberg, Chief-of-Operations of the German Tenth Panzer Division.

Back in the States that same day, the new Lieutenant General Fredendall was given a hero's welcome...

A COLONEL CALLS ON ROMMEL

'Mitgegangen, mitgefangen, mitgehangen.'
Old German Saying★

★*Gone with, caught with, hanged with.*

Chateau de la Roche-Guyon, France,
July 2nd 1944

The whores in the officers' brothel were dark, flashy, exotic. Lt. Colonel Scharf, who was with Captain Brandt and Lt. Hartmann, thought they didn't look German, as whores in an officers' brothel normally were, even here in France where there were good quality whores a-plenty, and who were prepared to do sexual tricks that no German whore would. All the same, he told himself as he sipped his 'seventy-five', named after a famous French cannon, a mixture of cognac and cheap champagne, they spoke perfect German, in the harsh, tough accent of Berlin Wedding, the capital's working-class district.

All the same, they had none of the cockiness of the typical Berlin working-class 'pavement pounder'. Indeed, they seemed overly polite to the civilians in Party uniform who were enjoying the delights of a 'French brothel', as they kept calling the run-down eighteenth-century country house, as if it were one of the Seven Wonders of the World.

They even curtsied to a pot-bellied *Kreisleiter*, who wore the 'War Service Cross' as his sole wartime decoration, and who was quite drunk for such an early hour.

The three old hares had been through a lot together since North Africa – Russia again, Finland, and, since the Regiment had become part of a regular infantry division, individual behind-the-line fighting on the Normandy front. Now that Caen had fallen and the *Wehrmacht* was preparing to fall back into Belgium and Luxemburg, they were here awaiting special orders from Army Command HQ itself. So as Scharf had warned the other two, both as worn and dirty as he was, 'Two drinks and then a bit of the two-backed beast. That's all, comrades. You know these rear-echelon stallions. They don't like us stinking front swine. And we don't want any trouble – *now.*' He had emphasized the 'now', and both of them knew why.

So they sipped their 'seventy-fives' carefully and watched the antics of their fellow officers, mostly other 'rear-echelon stallions' and civilians, one of whom had brought his secretary-mistress with him, and all of them knew why. 'Heaven, arse and cloudburst,' Hartmann, the ex-Legionnaire, had sneered. 'The fat bastard doesn't look as if he can get it up in the first place, and now he wants a whore and his little grey mouse* with him in bed as well. *Pfui*!'

But it was the drunken *Kreisleiter* with the War Service Cross who was making a real fool of himself that night. He had just slapped the fat Madam, bursting out of her tight black silk frock, across her corsetted buttocks, crying 'Champus – champus for everybody, especially our gallant soldiers from the front, Madam.' He indicated Scharf's little party.

'*Champus*!' the whores breathed with faked enthusiasm.

The brothel-keeper was not so enthusiastic. 'Can't give you that much champagne, *Kreisleiter*,' she said wearily. She tugged at her right breast, which appeared to have slipped out of her corset. 'We're running out of supplies ... since the Tommies and *Amis* have started advancing.'

The *Kreisleiter*'s drunken smile vanished as if by magic from his fat, well-fed face. 'Don't talk to me, a high Party official, like that, *Sarah*. One word from me and you could be going up the chimney tomorrow morning sharpish.' He thrust up his forefinger in a circling gesture, as if to indicate smoke rising.

Nickname for the German Army's female auxiliaries.

The colour fled from her cheeks. 'Yes, *Kreisleiter*, champus for everybody.'

The civilians cheered, and the whores, tough and hard-boiled though they were, suddenly looked very frightened. 'That's the way, *Kreisleiter*,' one of the civilians, a big, heavy-set middle-aged official who had Gestapo written all over him, shouted. 'Sugar and the whip, as the Führer used to say in the old days, that gets the hook-nosed swine working!'

Scharf frowned. Now he knew why the drunken Party official had called the Madam 'Sarah'. All female Jews had been ordered to use the supposed Hebrew name. She and the rest of her 'working girls', as she called them, were German Jews.

Now the cheap champagne started to flow. The whores hastened to appease the *Kreisleiter*. One of them took the *Kreisleiter's* sausage-like middle finger in her hands and dipped it a glass of champagne, and maintained that the distorted image represented the true size of his organ. That gave him a chance to boast drunkenly about what happened to 'wenches when I fuck 'em. They don't want any other man after that.'

Another girl, skinny unlike the others, and clad only in a black corset and laddered silk stockings, attempted to pull off the *Kreisleiter's* tight breeches to check the truth of the matter. The Madam joined in. Together, giggling dutifully with a well-concealed air of strain, they managed to get his tight breeches off. They were now playing with his flaccid organ, which lay limp and useless beneath a white mountain of hairless belly, while he laughed uproariously at their antics.

It was clear to the three ex-Brandenburgers that the coast was becoming clearer. Most of the officers who were not too drunk had vanished. They had abandoned the brothel to the working-class, upstart Party officials, who had come here from the Reich, their heads full of their provincial notions of naughty French whores and what they called, with a roll of their eyes, 'Oh, la, la'. 'It's about time, comrades,' Scharf whispered out of the side of his mouth not taking his gaze off the red-faced excited civilians for a moment, free hand gripping the butt of his pistol in his pocket and not the one in the holster. 'Pick your girls.'

They nodded their understanding, remembering their instruction that they had to find bedrooms facing the chateau, which was *his* private quarters.

Now as he clumped upstairs after the girl of his choice, Scharf felt a twinge of doubt. These girls were Jewish: they were too frightened to do anything but what the ex-Brandenburgers ordered them to do. Still, he could go through the motions with her. Her days of servicing German officers were soon to be over. The Tommies would be next. He wondered whether she had an English phrase book and was secretly learning the key words of her profession.

She opened the door of her dingy little room, with the red marks of the squashed bedbugs on the faded wall paper and the blackout curtains made of dyed Army blankets. Next to them there was a shabby jacket, adorned with the yellow star of David. He frowned momentarily. Then he let her get down to business, as he gazed over her shoulder at the chateau, where they were beginning to put up the blackout curtains. He nodded his approval. Things would be getting quieter – and the sentries would relax, now that the high-ranking staff and aides were safely tucked away inside their blacked-out headquarters.

She started to caress his clothed body. He didn't object. She opened his flies wordlessly, and took his hardening penis in her hands. He stiffened more. What a shitting world, he told himself a little bitterly. A front swine can't even get the dirty water off his chest in peace. Still, the sensation was very good. The girl knew her business. Perhaps she preferred him, as ragged and smelly as he was, to the Party bullies, most of them very drunk by now. God knows what they'd do to these women, especially as they knew they were Jews and no one would worry if they got hurt.

When she tried to take him in her mouth, he guided her lips away gently. He couldn't subject her to that; after all he was indirectly responsible for her being here, 'On top, please,' he said a little hoarsely.

'*Jawohl, Herr Oberst*,' she responded dutifully. Spreading her legs, she straddled him and began moving up and down, moaning as if she enjoyed it, though he knew she didn't. Within minutes it was all over. He would have dearly loved to have lain back on the rumpled bed and fallen asleep, but there was no time for that now. He pulled out his battered wallet and dropped a pile of greasy, worthless occupation marks on the night table. 'Thank you.'

She wiped between her legs and looked at him as if she were seeing him for the first time. It was obvious that most of her clients were not as polite as he was.

'Now,' he said carefully. 'I have a little present for you.'

'A present?' she echoed, caught completely off guard. 'A present for *me*?'

'Yes.' He pulled the tin out of his side pocket. 'A pound of genuine English tea. You can sell it on the black market. For something useful, instead of that dud money.'

Her eyes filled with tears. 'A present for me,' she repeated. 'Don't you know I'm Jewish, sir?'

He ignored the remark. 'For a favour, stay here, till I come back. If anyone knocks, tell them you're being paid for something a little extra. Clear?'

She nodded, lips moving as she repeated his instructions to herself, before saying yet again, 'A *present*...'

Exit from the lavatory window was easy. Even Hartmann, with his bulk and still stuffing his shirt back into his pants, managed it. The three of them dropped into the tight little alley behind the brothel. It stank of age, cat's piss and ancient lechery. They crept along the wall towards the Chateau de la Roche-Guyon. They knew exactly what to do. SS *Obergruppenführer* Dietrich of the SS Panzer Corps had briefed them perfectly. 'Colonel,' he had ended the briefing, 'bring me Rommel. Then we can act. That madman at Berchtesgaden has to be stopped before he ruins our Germany completely. Rommel is the only man that can do it. Good luck.'

Now, following Dietrich's instructions, they moved ever closer to the Chateau. Someone somewhere was playing Chopin on the place's grand piano. At any other time,

Scharf would have grinned. The place and the piano were typical; the staff, remote from the shooting war, loved to live. Even now with disaster looming in France, they were still enjoying a good war.

He found the cellar door. It was open, as Dietrich, who had once called the Führer by the familiar 'thou', had promised it would be. The hinges were even freshly oiled so that they made no noise. Everything, it seemed, had been planned, down to the smallest detail. Now the only imponderable was Rommel, who, according to Dietrich, spent this 'blue hour', as the French called it, by himself, alone in his study dealing with his correspondence and writing his daily letter to his beloved wife in far-off Swabia. How would he receive him, Scharf, after all this time since North Africa, and the invitation to high treason he brought with him?

They caught the Field Marshal completely by surprise. They slipped in through the side door, white and gilt, although it was obviously meant for the servants. He was crouched over his great eighteenth-century desk, wearing his glasses, in which he wouldn't be seen dead save by his intimates, busily writing at a pad of cheap Army notepaper, perhaps to his wife. But he reacted quickly as he felt the cooler air from outside play about the nape of his neck, where he had loosened his tight collar and the ribbon of the Knight's Cross which hung from it. With the speed of a much younger man, he grabbed the pistol which always lay on the desk in front of him these days and swung round in his swivel chair, safety catch off and ready for use on the intruder.

Hastily Scharf said, as the other two watched the servants' door behind him, 'It's all right, Field Marshal, we're friends. May I re-introduce myself? Scharf, formerly of the Brandenburg Regiment.'

Rommel took off his glasses. Slowly he said, 'Scharf, eh. Yes, I remember you – Kasserine and a lot earlier ... Dasburg on the Belgian frontier ... back in 'forty.' He put the pistol down. 'But you don't look very friendly, Scharf. Not in that filthy uniform.'

'Sir. Just come from the front.'

'I see. And you thought you'd just pop by your Supreme Commander and tell him you're safe, eh?' He gave a half-smile.

This night Scharf had no time for humour, even from the man he admired so much. Every minute he spent here, with what he knew now, meant he was in extreme danger. 'Sir, I'd like to talk to you under four eyes.'

Rommel laughed at the German expression for a personal conversation. 'Oh, yes, an army commander has not much to do these days with the Führer directing operations from Berchtesgaden. By all means, Scharf. Obviously I've got all the time in the world.'

Down below, the unknown pianist had changed from the rather sad Chopin to a lively selection of Lehar, and Rommel commented, 'See, I even have a lieutenant colonel of the Greater German General Staff to serenade me. All right, Scharf, fire away.'

Heartened by Rommel's last cynical remarks, Scharf took the plunge. 'Sir, you know the situation in France. You know, too, that if we – you – don't do something soon, the German Army in France will be wiped out. That will mean the end of the Reich. Our Germany will have nothing to bargain with. Why should the enemy give us anything when our army is destroyed?'

'Yes, I've already made that point to the Führer.'

'But the Führer won't listen, sir.' Scharf risked being arrested for defeatism and insulting the Führer on the spot, if Dietrich had misinterpreted the Field Marshal.

'I shall pretend that I have not heard that remark, Colonel Scharf,' Rommel said severely, but the latter could see that his words had hit home. For Rommel glanced suspiciously around the room, as if he half expected someone hidden behind the Gobelins to be listening to him. 'I take your point and agree with it. I know what your General

Dietrich wants of me. He wants me to use my good name with the enemy, especially Montgomery, to arrange a peace while there's still time, whether the Führer likes it or not. In short, you are expecting me to break my personal oath to the Führer and commit high treason, for which there is a little penalty – death by firing squad.'

Scharf wasn't put off his stroke by the words. Dietrich had briefed him well. After all, he knew the Führer better than all of them. Hadn't Dietrich marched at Hitler's side on the abortive Munich putsch back in 1923? 'General Dietrich has already broken *his* oath of loyalty, sir. And he has sent me to assure that you are safe from the Führer's revenge – and the Gestapo.'

'How?'

'You are to be brought to his headquarters and protected by the men of his own SS Panzer Corps, sir.'

'But most of them are young men, fanatical National Socialists. They know nothing else but the Nazi creed. Hitler is their idol.'

'General Dietrich will vouch for their loyalty, sir. As he has already told you, sir, I believe, he will carry out every order you issue implicitly, and his officers and men will do the same – or else.'

What followed seemed to last for ever. In the corner, the great nineteenth-century grandfather clock ticked away the seconds of their lives with metallic inexorability. Down below, the pianist still hammered away at his Lehar tunes. Rommel stared at the letter to his wife and young son, and somehow, Scharf guessed what he was thinking. If he defected now, his wife and son would pay the penalty. It was the latest piece of Nazi blackmail. Any soldier who deserted, defected or expressed defeatism at the front where Hitler's thugs couldn't reach him would know that there was one sure and cruel way of making him toe the line. His family. They would be arrested on a count of treachery, not theirs, but his. In due course, they would be sent to a concentration camp, and perhaps to their deaths. What decent man could attempt to defy the regime under those circumstances?

Without waiting for Rommel's decision, Scharf played his last card – the great secret which the old party bully-boy Dietrich had only imparted to him after a great deal of deliberation. 'Sir, a certain Colonel von Stauffenberg—'

'I know him. Badly wounded just before we left Africa. Lost an eye and an arm, too, if I'm not mistaken. But carry on, Colonel.'

'Well, sir, General Dietrich informs me that he will make an attempt on the Führer's life before the month's out ... even if he loses his own in the assassination attempt.'

'So?' Rommel asked, no emotion revealed in his manner and tone.

'It will be the signal, sir.'

'For civil war in the Reich?' Rommel said coldly.

'No sir. But for a take-over of power from the Party by the Army and a speedy approach to the Allies to make peace. Everyone's in it, sir. Army, Navy, Air Force, even the Armed SS.' He looked expectantly at the Field Marshal. But Rommel's face revealed nothing, except perhaps a little cold disdain. Finally he said, 'Have you ever thought, Colonel, that Hitler may be more dangerous dead than alive?'

It was a remark that puzzled Scharf. If he had lived longer, he might have understood it, but unfortunately for the Brandenburger, that was not going to be the case.

Rommel forced a smile. 'I see the thought means little to you, Colonel. No matter. Perhaps I shall find time some day to explain it to you.' He shrugged. 'Perhaps not. Now tell Dietrich I am considering the matter and will contact him when I'm ready.'

'But sir—'

Rommel held up his hand for silence. 'You are a brave young man and you have served me loyally. I don't want you to risk your life on my account any further. You must go now. I am surrounded by spies. This is about the only time I can be by myself unobserved. But soon it will be time for dinner, and then they will come. They must not find you here, Scharf. It would be dangerous – very dangerous – for both of us. Now go.'

Scharf hesitated, then thought better of it. After all, Rommel was a German field marshal, and one didn't disobey the commands of a German field marshal. He clicked stiffly to attention and raised his hand to his battered cap in salute.

Rommel nodded in acknowledgement and turned back to the papers on his ornate writing desk, as if Scharf had already departed.

They returned by the same route as they had entered. Now the pianist had ceased playing, and although the Field Marshal had just said that dinner would be served soon, there were no sounds from the chateau's kitchen. Scharf, however, was too concerned with getting back to his vehicle behind the officers' brothel to note the silent warnings. It was an oversight he wouldn't live to regret.

They came out into the gravelled drive close to the ornate chateau gardens. Suddenly there was a footfall close by – and another. A harsh voice cried from the darkness, '*Stehenbleiben – Geheime Staatspolizei!*'

Even before Scharf felt a sense of impending disaster at the Gestapo man's order,

Hartmann reacted. He fired blind. Someone cried in pain. Next moment, a body crashed to the gravel, and firing broke out. 'Run for it,' Scharf ordered, though he already realized that there wasn't much hope for them. There were dark shapes suddenly everywhere in the gardens firing from behind the ornamental shrubs and carefully tended dwarf trees.

Still, he knew it was really 'march or croak' now. He pulled out the pistol he kept in his pocket. It fired dum-dum bullets, for use in a dire emergency such as this. The tip of each bullet was criss-crossed with deep grooves. When the slug struck a body, the bullet shattered outwards and caused a tremendous wound, much larger than that of the ordinary bullet. Anyone hit by a dum-dum bullet went down and stayed down. Crouched low, he advanced, firing to left and right. Gestapo agents went down everywhere, a couple of them being swept completely off their feet by the tremendous impact of the doctored bullets. But there seemed ever more of them.

Brandt was the first to go down. With his one arm, combat-experienced as he had become over the last year, he wasn't as agile as the other two. He cried out as he crumpled to the gravel, hit in the stomach.

Hartmann turned to help him. 'Hans, no,'

Brandt yelled urgently. 'Leave me ... please.'

'I'm coming!'

'*NO* ... no use.' Brandt put his pistol to his head. Scharf, just behind, gasped with horror, as Brandt pressed the trigger before Hartmann could reach him. The side of his head flew off in a welter of red gore, through which the shattered bone gleamed in the new moon like polished ivory. Next instant Hartmann went down on his knees, his chest ripped apart by a burst of Schmeisser fire. Still, like a boxer refusing to go down for a count of ten, he kept on firing, growing weaker by the instant as the blood dripped from what looked like a series of bloody buttonholes stitched across his broad chest. *Click.* His magazine was empty. With the last of his strength, an angry Hartmann threw the useless weapon at the nearest Gestapo man. He missed.

A helpless Scharf crouched low, feeding a new magazine into his own pistol, and fired to left and right once again, keeping the police at bay. His mind raced wildly. What in three devils' name was he going to do? Should he abandon Hartmann, who had been with him right from the start? How many such moments had they fought together, moments when there had seemed to have been no hope? Yet they had survived all the same. Was this one of them?

The bullet hit him like a blow from a great, cruel club. It caught him in the small of the back. He gasped, all breath knocked out of his body. He went down on his knees, struggling for breath like an ancient asthmatic in the throes of a fatal final attack. Bravely he fought to rise. To no avail. Close behind, his unseen assailant fired again and struck him in the right shoulder. He yelled with the sheer agony of it. The pistol dropped from suddenly nerveless fingers.

'All right, you treacherous scum, raise your hands.' It was the voice of the Gestapo man in the leather coat from the officers' brothel. They had walked straight into a trap. Someone had blabbed. Perhaps one of Dietrich's fanatical young SS officers? Not that it mattered now. He was finished, he knew that. Hartmann was perhaps already dead. Brandt was dead. Now it was his turn. He couldn't be taken alive. He had heard about the Gestapo and their sadistic methods. They'd keep him alive till he revealed what he knew – and that meant betraying the Field Marshal.

Suddenly, completely out of the blue, that terrible pain forgotten for a moment, he remembered that first day back on the River Our at Dasburg, back in May 1940, in what seemed now another age. The peasant girl in the patched white cotton knickers ... the abrupt stand-to ... the strange general staring down at the river and the heights of Belgium beyond ... the corporal on the motor bike and his cheeky reply: 'I hardly know it myself ... Flying frigging Rommel...' Scharf smiled weakly at the memory. He had been happy then, when it had all started, with what he thought was a whole, long, exciting life in front of him, war as a great adventure ... He gasped for breath, feeling the life ebb out of him. A dark mist threatened to overcome him. He shook his head to fight it off, and wished the next instant that he hadn't. The pain was terrible.

'All right, scum,' the Gestapo repeated. Now the man in the leather coat was standing directly behind him. He could hear his coat creak.

Weakly Scharf sought his other pistol, the one he had kept in its holster. He didn't manage it. A hard, steel-shod boot crushed his right hand. He sobbed with pain and stopped.

The Gestapo bent down. Scharf could smell the beer on his breath. Something cold and metallic pressed itself to the base of his skull behind his right ear. He tried to wriggle his head away from it. He knew what was coming. In vain. The Gestapo man was too strong for him. 'Traitor,' the man hissed, voice full of hate. 'Traitor to our holy Fatherland.'

'I did my duty—' Colonel Scharf never finished. The pistol exploded. The whole rear of his skull lifted up from his spine. The Gestapo man cursed as his prized leather coat was showered with the dead traitor's blood. 'This bastard's dead, too,' he called to his comrades. 'That's the lot ... Let's get back into the knocking shop and have a drink ... Then we'll deal with the Yid gash.'

Up in the chateau, the unknown pianist started to play again. It would soon be time for the Field Marshal's dinner...

ENVOI

'Above all I must demand from my officers that they set an example and obey.'
Field Marshal Rommel to General Brauchitsch, 1941

I was back in the UK when we found out what had happened to the one-time 'Desert Fox'. It had been a long, painful progress, but they hadn't managed to save my leg. So they had fitted me up with what I call still, all these years later, 'my peg-leg', though it isn't, of course, and had taught me to walk again. God, one doesn't know how hopeless one feels with one leg. Anyway, I was beginning to walk quite well again when I heard the first news of Rommel since he had first disappeared from the German 'order-of-battle', as we called it, some time in the summer of 1944 in France.

Apparently, some time in the October of that year, Hitler decided that Rommel had been behind the plotters who had tried to assassinate him on July 20th, 1944. But the one-time 'people's hero' wouldn't be strung up and strangled by chicken wire, with the strangulation being shot by cameras for the Führer's sadistic entertainment later. Rommel would be allowed the officer-and-gentleman's way out. He would be allowed to commit suicide, and then his death was to be hushed up as 'due to natural causes'. Not even Rommel's beloved wife, Lucie, was to be told what really happened. There was to be no blemish on Rommel's career.

While Rommel recovered from the wounds he had suffered in an RAF aerial attack in France at the small 'villa' he owned at a place in Swabia, the village of Herrlingen (it's still there, apparently), the men who were privy to the plot to get rid of Rommel prepared with German thoroughness. There was even a study group under a lieutenant-colonel, called 'Study Group F', which drafted a programme entitled 'Sequence for a State Funeral (R). All the detailed draft lacked was the date and place where Rommel's funeral was to take place. That was soon to be rectified.

On October 12, 1944, an old friend of Rommel's, a heavy-drinking, red-faced general named Burgdorf, came to see Rommel at Herrlingen. Alone with the Field Marshal in the latter's study, he destroyed Rommel's hopes that he would not suffer as his fellow conspirators had. Burgdorf, a little drunk, though not showing it said, 'You have been accused of complicity in the plot on Hitler's life'. Thereupon Burgdorf reeled off a list of fellow officers, now in Gestapo prisons, who had testified against the Field Marshal.

Rommel's fate was sealed.

According to various sources that came to light afterwards, Rommel went to pieces for a little while and asked for a few moments to think over the consequences of Burgdorf's statement, especially now, when he knew what the Führer expected him to do if the matter was to be hushed up and Lucie to be given a field marshal's pension for the rest of her days.

Finally he asked Burgdorf, who was probably longing for a stiff drink, 'Can I take your car, Burgdorf, and drive off quietly somewhere. But I'm not sure that I can trust myself to handle a pistol properly.'

But even that eventuality had been taken care of. 'We have brought a preparation with us,' Burgdorf replied. He meant poison. If the Field Marshal couldn't shoot himself, he *could* take poison. The main thing was he did as Hitler wanted. With the *Wehrmacht* fighting desperately on both the Eastern and Western Front, the Führer wanted no scandals that might demoralize the army even further. Rommel had to die the hero he had always been.

Outside, as Rommel left the house, his poise restored, carrying his bejewelled Field Marshal's staff given to him by Hitler personally in what now seemed another age, it was a fine autumn day. He remembered he still had his house keys in his pocket.

In a gesture which I have always thought typical of German provincial small-mindedness, he handed them over to his sixteen-year-old son, who was already in uniform. Then, together with Burgdorf, he entered the latter's Opel and they drove off in the direction of the next village. Somewhere along that village road, fringed by autumnal trees at their finest, Rommel, unable to shoot himself, accepted the poison given to him by Burgdorf. Later, long afterwards, the Opel's driver would testify that on returning to the car, he saw that the Field Marshal was obviously dying. 'He (Rommel) was unconscious, slumped down and sobbing – not a death rattle or groaning, but sobbing. His cap had fallen off. I sat him upright and put his cap back on again...'

In the years since I first learned of the manner of Rommel's death, I have always been moved by that gesture of a common soldier. He wanted the Field Marshal to die like the soldier he had always been. Naturally, back in 1945 when we first heard of the Fox's' death, we didn't know such details. Indeed, as far as the world was concerned, Rommel had been forgotten. It was just a small item at the bottom of the *Daily Express* third page – 'Jerry Field Marshal Committed Suicide' – and that was about it.

A couple of the other 'cripples', as we called ourselves, who wore the 'Africa Star' with the '8' of the Eighth Army, looked a bit thoughtful. One of them – a handsome captain who looked a bit like poor old 'Cherry-picker' I once knew – limped off and sat by himself on the bench there, alone with his thoughts, staring at nothing. I thought of going over to him and saying something, but I didn't think it was wise to do so, in the end. If he was moved, what could I say? After all, he had been the enemy for two long years. Besides, he was a 'Jerry', a 'Kraut', a 'Hun', and we'd all had a bellyful of Germans...

Professor 'Crasher' Nichols, M.C.